To Marvin Monette

July 26 – 1946

Rev. Wm A. Pagley

THE GOOD BAD BOY

BY GERALD T. BRENNAN
Angel City
Angel Food
The Man Who Dared a King
The Ghost of Kingdom Come
For Heaven's Sake

THE GOOD BAD BOY

The Diary of an Eighth-Grade Boy

REV. GERALD T. BRENNAN

THE BRUCE PUBLISHING COMPANY
MILWAUKEE

Nihil obstat: WILLIAM F. BERGAN, Censor Deputatus
Imprimatur: ✠ JAMES E. KEARNEY
Feast of the Guardian Angels, 1941

(Fifth Printing — 1945)

This book is complete and unabridged and is reprinted in full
accord with the rules and regulations of the War Production
Board for the conservation of paper and other materials.

To
The Dunlapers

IDENTIFICATION

Name ..... *Pompey Briggs* .....

Residence *17 Putnam St., Blackford, N.Y.*

Age ..... *13 years* .....

Height ..... *5 feet, 3 inches* .....

Weight ..... *118 pounds* .....

Color of Eyes ..... *Blue* .....

Hair ..... *Brown* .....

Collar ..... *14* .....

Shoes ..... *7½* .....

In case of illness or accident, notify

Name ..... *Mr. Chester Briggs* .....

Residence *17 Putnam St., Blackford, N.Y.*

Phone ..... *Main 375* .....

Tomorrow I shall enter the eighth grade of Holy Cross School, and I have just been thinking. . . . Great men always keep diaries. Perhaps, that's what makes them great.
If I keep a diary, I, too, may become great. Who knows?

Pompey Briggs

TUESDAY, September 6

Went to Mass this morning, and then went to school. Am in the eighth grade now. Three new pupils in our class — one of them is a girl. Everybody was dressed up today. Mom let me wear my long pants, because you have to look big in the eighth grade. No school this afternoon. Clara let me take her bike, and Bo and I went for a ride. Sure enough, I had a puncture. It took Bo and me an hour to fix it. I'll never hear the end of that puncture. I think girls are about the meanest things in the world, and anyone who has a sister will say the same thing.

WEDNESDAY, September 7

Looks as though this teacher means business. Her name is Sister Agnes. The new pupils are Timothy O'Malley, Walter Dickson, and Jean Wallace. Jean must be smart, because she had her hand up most of the time. Mom baked some oatmeal cookies today. Cookies always come in handy after a hard day's work.

9

The man came to paper my room. The bed's down, so I'll have to sleep with the mattress on the floor. Wish we'd paper every day, because I like sleeping on the floor.

THURSDAY, September 8
Sister Agnes gave us our regular seats today. Bo is in the front row. Terry is on the side. Froggie is near a window. Mine is a dandy — the one over in the corner. The Wallace girl sits across from me. Hope she's good in arithmetic. Clara is still talking about that puncture. That's the girl of it. You'd think that I did it on purpose. My room isn't finished yet, so I'll sleep on the floor again tonight.

FRIDAY, September 9
Clint Tucker had a new haircut. Boy, did he yell when someone hit him in the neck with a rubber band! I wonder why teachers make such a fuss over little things. Aunt Sarah was over tonight. Couldn't listen to the radio, because Mom and Aunt Sarah were talking. The papering is done but the bed isn't up. So back to the floor again tonight. What a life! Just like being in the army.

SATURDAY, September 10
Had to cut the grass this morning. After dinner Froggie and I went to see "The Stolen Coin" and "Silver Wings." Saw "The Stolen Coin" twice and was late for supper. Wish Clara would mind her own business

when Mom and Pop are mad. She makes them think about things they would never think about themselves. Heard all about the puncture again, and had to do the dishes alone. No more sleeping on the floor.

SUNDAY, September 11
When I'm President, I'll make all days just like today. After Mass Pop took the family to Uncle Harry's farm. Clara and I hunted forty-seven eggs and then went horseback riding. I can hardly sit down tonight. Had chicken and apple pie for dinner. Aunt Kate gave me two pieces of the pie. You certainly can enjoy your dinner when you know that you won't have to wash the dishes. All dishes should be washed by women. Uncle Harry gave me a puppy with white feet and a white nose. Mom made me fix a bed for the dog in the cellar. Think I'll call him "Boots," but will ask the gang first. Mom said that farms are pretty nice things except that they're always in the country.

MONDAY, September 12
The dog cried all night. Mom blamed me. Could I help it if the dog was lonesome? "Boots" as a name is out. Froggie wants to call him "Peanuts." Bo wants "Pepper." Jean Wallace wants "Cider," and "Cider" will be his name.

TUESDAY, September 13
Cider cried again last night. This morning Mom and Pop looked daggers at me. Of course, Clara had to in-

terfere. Girls certainly give me a headache. I sneaked Cider up the back stairs and he'll sleep with me tonight. After all, pals should be together.

WEDNESDAY, September 14
Plenty happened today. Mom was mad because Cider put his dirty feet on my sheets. Every time I try to be kind to somebody, I get into trouble. Certainly Cider didn't get the sheets dirty on purpose. Cider isn't used to sleeping on sheets. Sent to bed early. Asked God tonight to keep Cider from crying. Hope God was listening.

THURSDAY, September 15
God was listening to my prayers last night, because Cider didn't cry. Everybody was happy today. That's the way it should be. When everything is all right around this house, then I begin to worry. It's a sure sign that something must be wrong.

FRIDAY, September 16
Had medical inspection in school today. When the nurse put the stick on Terry's tongue, he couldn't say "Ah," because he has bad tonsils. Ray Perkins needs glasses. The doctor said that I have one bad tooth. Bet anything that Mom will take me to the dentist on a Saturday. That's the way they do things around this house. Bought a rubber ball for Cider. Cut the grass after school. Froggie, Terry, and I are going to caddy at Lake Shore Country Club tomorrow.

SATURDAY, September 17

Poured rain all day. Cutting the grass yesterday was wasted effort.

SUNDAY, September 18

Pop took the family for a ride this afternoon. Had to sit in the back seat with Mom. Clara sat with Pop — proving again that this is a woman's world. Stopped at Aunt Kate's for a long time. After two hours of waiting, Aunt Kate gave me an apple. What good are apples except when they're in pies? Supper at home.

MONDAY, September 19

Was sent to the Principal for not having homework. Father Foley begged me off and sent me on an errand. Had fire drill this afternoon. I'm not wishing anything bad, but some time it would be nice to have a fire drill that wasn't a false alarm. Imagine not having to go to school! Suppose they'd get around it some way. Mom went to a card party tonight and Pop went to a meeting. Clara and I made fudge which stuck to the pan as usual.

TUESDAY, September 20

Lots of excitement at Terry's house today. Mr. Mann called Mom early this morning. Mom was gone all day, and now Terry has a baby sister. Supper was late because Mom was over at Mann's. Can't understand why Mom should spend the whole day just looking at a new baby. Pop is beginning to like Cider — meaning the dog.

WEDNESDAY, September 21

Traded my combination pen and pencil for Clint Tucker's pocketknife. Walked home with Jean Wallace and carried her books. I'm squeezing for the Yankees to win the pennant. Jean hopes that the Yankees will win too.

THURSDAY, September 22

Had spelling contest today. Girls won. Anyway, Presidents don't have to worry about spelling because their secretaries spell the words for them. Sister read us the story about "Horatio at the Bridge." Bill Carroll took Clara to a dance tonight. Can't a sister be nice when a boy friend comes to the house? I could tell Bill Carroll more about Clara in five minutes than he'll ever learn about her in a million years. When I'm in high school, I'll be going to dances too.

FRIDAY, September 23

Froggie, Terry, Bo, and I formed a Club — "The Beaver Chiefs Social Club." Nobody will be allowed into meetings except members. The password is "Snicklefritz." Dues will be a nickel a week. If we get enough money, we'll go camping next summer. We can't have meetings in Froggie's cellar because it's too small. Bo's mother doesn't believe in clubs, so we can't have our meetings there. Terry's woodshed would be a swell place, but Terry is afraid that we'll disturb the baby. Pop doesn't know it, but meetings will be held in our garage. Froggie is treasurer and guards the money. Bo was elected secretary. Terry was elected vice-president. I was elected president. I knew I'd be president of something some day.

SATURDAY, September 24
The Beaver Chiefs wanted to have a meeting this morning, but no luck. Pop spoiled everything by spending most of the morning in the garage, and we had no other place to meet. Pop and I went uptown this afternoon and Pop bought a new shirt. Pancakes for supper.

SUNDAY, September 25
Jean Wallace looked pretty nice this morning in her new hat and I told her so. Rained all afternoon. Counted the money in my bank. Have thirty-eight cents. No company. Still raining.

MONDAY, September 26
The Yankees won today. Bet Jean is happy. I know I am. School was just school today, if you know what I mean. I can't see why we have to learn the cost of carpeting and papering a room. When I'm President, I won't have to worry about such things. Schools don't care what they teach as long as they have something to teach. Cider tore the parlor curtain and Pop locked him in the cellar for being a bad boy.

TUESDAY, September 27

A day of sorrow! Woke up with a toothache but went to school. Mom took me to the dentist this afternoon. Dentist pulled the tooth. Have the tooth wrapped in cotton so that the Beaver Chiefs can see it tomorrow. Mom said that if a dog finds my tooth and swallows it, then all of my teeth will grow in crooked. I don't want that to happen.

WEDNESDAY, September 28

The Beaver Chiefs had their first meeting today. Bo stood at the door of the garage and received the password as each one entered. Froggie almost forgot the password. I tried to make a speech but no one would listen. Everybody talked at the same time. After we make the rules, things will be better. We're going to make Cider our mascot.

THURSDAY, September 29

Everybody wants to join the Beaver Chiefs. New members will have to pass an initiation which will be done by us. We made a rule that, whenever a member owes a quarter for dues, he will be expelled from the club. Any member expelled from the club can't go camping next summer.

FRIDAY, September 30

Arithmetic exam this morning. Forgot the rules for carpeting and papering and made a mess of the whole thing. Put the carpet where the paper should have been. English exam this afternoon. Could get only 148 words for the 200-word composition. Percents will go on the monthly reports. When I'm President, I'll make a law forbidding all examinations in schools. Examinations were invented by lazy teachers. Whenever teachers are tired or lazy, they give examinations. After all, teachers are hired to teach. Watch me put an end to examinations!

SATURDAY, October 1

The Beaver Chiefs went caddying today. Froggie caddied for a man who swore every time his ball rolled into the sand — just as if Froggie could help it. I caddied for a gentleman. Every time he made a poor shot he asked me what was wrong. I answered right back: "Mister, you peeked. Keep your head down!" All caddies say that. Earned a dollar and a quarter. Walked twelve miles, maybe a hundred. Can't see why golfers have to use so many clubs. Arrived home at seven-thirty. Mom was mad because she wanted to go to the movies for the first show. Going to bed early because my feet hurt.

SUNDAY, October 2

Sweet potatoes for dinner. For me all potatoes should be sweet potatoes. Pop took the family for a ride to the Fish Hatcheries. Stopped to watch a ball game — Pembroke against Williamson. Pembroke won. Pop treated us to ice cream. Boy, oh boy, the Yankees won the pennant. World Series will start Wednesday. Watch my Yankees beat the Cincinnati Reds! Fried sweet potatoes for supper. Pompey Briggs goes to bed tonight with a stomach full of sweet potatoes.

MONDAY, October 3

Reports today. When Father Foley left the room, Sister Agnes made me go out into the hall. Sister Agnes told Father Foley that I was not working hard, and Father Foley said plenty. Bo passed and so did Froggie. Terry half-passed: he went down in arithmetic. Waited until after supper before showing the report to Mom and Pop. Pop was mad and said that I had disgraced the Briggs family. Right in the middle of everything Clara told about the Beaver Chiefs having meetings in the garage. Pop said that there would be no more meetings, and that I couldn't be a Beaver Chief unless I improved. But I must be a Beaver Chief because I'm the president. Mom made me study carpeting and papering tonight. Cider knew that something was wrong because he kept rubbing my leg under the table. That's loyalty.

TUESDAY, October 4

Sister changed some seats today. She tried to put me in the second seat but my legs were too long for the small seat. Back I went to my seat in the corner. Gave the Beaver Chiefs the bad news about no more meetings in our garage. Froggie is going to try to have the meetings in his cellar even though the cellar is small.

WEDNESDAY, October 5

Writing teacher visited the school today. She sat in the seat with me while I wrote the exercises. With thirty-six pupils in the room, why did she have to sit with me? Some women don't know their place. Bought Cider a collar for a dime. That leaves twenty-eight cents in my bank. The Beaver Chiefs are still without a meeting place. Froggie is waiting to catch his mother in good humor. World Series opened today and the Yankees won. Must have been a good game because the score was 2 to 1.

THURSDAY, October 6

Froggie's mother said that we could have our meetings in her cellar. After cleaning the cellar, we had a meeting. All members paid their dues. Now have twenty cents in the treasury. Froggie's mother will hold the money. Some day when Froggie's mother is not at home, Bill Lenox and Dave Wright will be initiated into the Beaver Chiefs. Mom and Clara have gone to the movies tonight — free dishes to ladies on Thursday nights. That means that we'll have two new dishes in the house by midnight. The Yankees won their second game. No game tomorrow.

FRIDAY, October 7

History test today. Suppose Sister Agnes was tired again. Beats all how teachers can find excuses to have tests. Never yet met a teacher who wouldn't have a test at the drop of a hat. No wonder we get "athletes' thumb"; we write too much. Just as the Beaver Chiefs were having a meeting, the fire autos tore down the street. Conway's house was on fire. Lots of fun watching the firemen climb ladders. Mom invited Mrs. Conway and Ted for supper. Mrs. Conway will sleep in our spare room. Ted will sleep with me.

SATURDAY, October 8
Big piece in the paper about the Conway fire. Mom helped Mrs. Conway clean her house. Most of the fire was upstairs. All of us feel sorry for Ted so we're going to make him a Beaver Chief without initiation. Clara cooked our meals and burnt the lamb chops. Looks as though the Yankees will run away with the series. Listened to the game over the radio and what a game! Score was 7 to 3. I'll bet that the Cincinnati Reds are pretty gloomy tonight. Hope my Yankees win tomorrow and everything will be over.

SUNDAY, October 9
Today was Mom's and Pop's Wedding Anniversary. Nineteen years is a long time to be married. I wasn't at the wedding because I'm only thirteen. Listened to the ball game over the radio, and boy, how my Yankees played ball! Reds were ahead at the end of the seventh inning, but we tied them in the ninth. And then, what a tenth inning! We scored three runs and the Reds couldn't touch us. Final score was 7 to 4 and my Yankees are the champions. Yankees certainly meant

business to finish the series in four straight games. Phoned Jean after the game and she was very happy. Aunt Kate and Uncle Harry came for supper. Mom almost kicked my leg off when I spilled the beets on the clean tablecloth. Why do women always serve beets when they have a clean tablecloth? I wonder.

MONDAY, October 10

After supper Mom tried on her new dress. Cider barked when he saw it. While Mom was admiring herself, Father Foley called at the house. He was taking the census and asked Pop a lot of questions. Saw Father Foley blow six smoke rings with one of Pop's cigars. Father Foley told Mom that I would have to study hard if I want to graduate. Mom was glad that she was wearing her new dress when Father Foley called. After all, what does Father Foley care about a new dress?

TUESDAY, October 11

History was great today: we had Paul Revere's ride. Bet Paul would be pretty good in a Western picture. Froggie's mother went uptown, so the Beaver Chiefs initiated Bill Lenox and Dave Wright. Dave certainly looked funny after we painted the skull and crossbones on his stomach. We blindfolded Bill Lenox, fed him castor oil, and put pepper in his nose. In the midst of the excitement Froggie's mother walked down the stairs and chased us out of the cellar. She said that our actions were disgraceful, and that there would be no more meetings of the Beaver Chiefs in her cellar.

She called us a pack of Indians. I suppose that Beaver Chiefs does sound kind of Indianish.

WEDNESDAY, October 12
Columbus Day! No school. The Beaver Chiefs had a sausage roast at Landon's Grove. Wish Columbus had discovered America more than once, because the Beaver Chiefs could stand a few more holidays. While we were at Landon's Grove, Mrs. Wright told Mom that the Beaver Chiefs painted Dave's stomach. Of course, Mom blamed me, because I'm the President of the Beaver Chiefs. Presidents have to take the thorns with the roses.

THURSDAY, October 13
Father Foley gave us a talk today and said that it's a sin to damage another's person or property. Wonder if Mrs. Wright told Father Foley about the initiation! Mom met Mrs. Wallace at the grocery store and they talked for a long time. Some day Mrs. Wallace may be one of our relatives. Mom and Clara have gone to the movies for more dishes.

FRIDAY, October 14
Pancakes for supper. If there's anything that I like better than pancakes, it must be sweet potatoes.

SATURDAY, October 15
Received a letter addressed to "Mr. Pompey Briggs." Here's what it said:

DEAR POMPEY:

Your presence is requested at a Halloween Party to be given by Miss Jean Wallace at her home, 348 Harris Street, on the night of Halloween at eight o'clock. Ghosts will sail through the clouds and hold court in the Wallace cellar. Please come in appropriate costume.

R.S.V.P.   JEAN WALLACE

Mom said that the "R.S.V.P." means that I'll have to write Jean and tell her that I'll be present. I liked the "Mr." on the envelope. People certainly look up to presidents.

SUNDAY, October 16

Spent two hours this afternoon composing letters to Jean. Finally decided on the following:

DEAR MISS WALLACE:

I take my pen in hand to inform you that I shall be present at your party on the night of Halloween. My costume will fit the occasion.

> Your sincere admirer,
> POMPEY BRIGGS
> *President of the Beaver Chiefs*

Put the stamp upside down and mailed the letter tonight.

MONDAY, October 17

Jean Wallace smiled at me several times today. Never

23

let on that I received the invitation, because I want her to get my answer in the mail. Maybe she's reading it now. Terry and Bo received invitations. Froggie was skipped. Think I'll go to the party dressed like a pirate and scare the girls. Won't have to bring a present, because this won't be a birthday party. That's why I never like birthday parties.

TUESDAY, October 18

Cider was sick today. Wouldn't drink his milk or eat his hamburg. Mom held his mouth while I poured in two spoonfuls of mineral oil. That should make him better. The Beaver Chiefs wanted to have a meeting tonight, but we had no place to meet. Anyway, Ted Conway and Froggie had to stay after school. We can't have meetings unless all members are present. For Jean's party Mom wants me to dress like George Washington, but who wants to wear those short pants? The gang would call me "sissy pants" and the President of the Beaver Chiefs is no "sissy pants."

WEDNESDAY, October 19

Cider was better today. Pop was madder than a wet hen tonight. A policeman gave him a ticket for parking his car too close to a hydrant. Pop had to go to the police station and pay two dollars. Mom was mortified. She said that she would expect something like that from me, but not from Pop. Pop looked pretty sheepish as he buried himself in the evening paper. I wanted the funnies but was afraid to ask for them. Haven't decided what I'll wear to Jean's party. I am still without a costume and the Beaver Chiefs are still without a meeting place.

THURSDAY, October 20

English class was great today. Sister read *The Man Without a Country*. Boy, that Philip Nolan certainly spoke out of turn. Told the story to Pop tonight and Pop made a speech. "Pomp," he said, "that story has a lesson for everybody — respect for the government. We live in a pretty good country. The least we can do is to say 'thanks' by being loyal to the flag. That's where Philip Nolan made his mistake." Pop's right. You can't fool with the government. Boy, I'm glad I live in the United States. Why, if I lived in some other country, I wouldn't be President of the Beaver Chiefs, and I wouldn't know Jean Wallace. Mom and Clara have gone to the movies for more dishes.

FRIDAY, October 21

Bellow Shaffer sprinkled sneezing powder on the floor this afternoon. What a riot of sneezes, especially from Nancy Bauer! Sister Agnes sent for the Principal and the class heard plenty. My fingers still ache from the task. Nobody would tell on Bellow, because we're always hearing about honor, and the eighth grade is just full of honor. Walked home with Jean. There will be sixteen at Jean's party. Bet I'll have the most fun because Jean is going to be my girl. Yes, Jean *is* my girl but nobody knows it.

SATURDAY, October 22

Rained all day and had to stay in the house. Have decided to go to Jean's party as an Indian. Clara shortened an old pair of Pop's pants to fit me. She sewed colored cloth on the sides and they look just like Indian pants. Will use a piece of rope for a belt. My brown shirt with some of Clara's beads around my neck, will make me look like a real Indian. Aunt Sarah is going to have chicken for dinner tomorrow and she promised to save the feathers for my headgear. Sneaked Pop's small hatchet out of the cellar and hid it in my bureau drawer. Believe me, this party will be something, and the President of the Beaver Chiefs will be some Indian.

SUNDAY, October 23

Mom invited Mrs. Conway and Ted for dinner. Mom certainly spread herself, and I spread myself about ten inches eating sweet potatoes. That's another law that I'm going to make. When I'm President, I'll make all farmers grow nothing but sweet potatoes. That ought to make a lot of friends for me. After dinner Ted and I went to a football game. Passed Jean's house but didn't see anybody.

MONDAY, October 24

Boy, did our house smell great today! Mom made ketchup. To me ketchup-making time is the best smelling time of the year. Some day Mom will be making ketchup in the White House. When visitors at the White House smell Mom's ketchup, the whole world will know that Mrs. Chester Briggs, mother of President Pompey Briggs, is the best cook in the world.

TUESDAY, October 25
Tom Larkin has joined the Beaver Chiefs. Mrs. Larkin said that we could hold meetings in her cellar, so Tom became a member without being initiated. Mrs. Larkin said that she thought it was a fine idea for boys to have a club. Mrs. Larkin treated the Beaver Chiefs to cider and doughnuts, so we decided to have our meetings more often. Pop calls the Beaver Chiefs "The Crime Club," and says that we'll never amount to anything. Mom met Mrs. Wallace uptown. Mrs. Wallace was buying things for the party, which promises to be *the* social event of our neighborhood. I'm going to do my part to make it a success.

WEDNESDAY, October 26
It never rains but it pours. Received an invitation from Virginia Drake to attend her Halloween party on the same night as Jean's. It just goes to show that, when you are president of something, you have lots of friends. Hate to disappoint Virginia because Virginia is my second best girl. Why do my two best girls have to have parties on the same night? Guess I'll tell Virginia that I'm engaged. Hope she won't think that I'm going to get married.

THURSDAY, October 27

Father Foley told us about the Mass today. It was a pretty good instruction. He showed us the vestments and his gold chalice. No one can touch the chalice except a holy person. Gee, Father Foley certainly knows lots of things. Hope I grow up to be like Father Foley. God never makes a mistake when He picks a priest, does He? God did an extra-special job when He picked Father Foley. To me Father Foley is tops.

FRIDAY, October 28

Sister Agnes was tired today, so we had a test. Wrote a composition about Philip Nolan and his trouble with the government. The Beaver Chiefs had another meeting tonight, but there were no doughnuts and cider. I was never so hungry and dry as I was during that meeting. Offered it up for the Poor Souls just as Father Foley told us to do. Mom had codfish and baked potatoes for supper. You ought to see Cider eat codfish; he loves it. Tried on my Indian suit tonight, took my hatchet, and put on a war dance. Pop yelled at me to stop. And when Pop yells, I stop.

SATURDAY, October 29

Rented Clara's bicycle for a quarter and the Beaver Chiefs went chestnutting. A farmer chased us. Tore my pants jumping over a fence. Mom was mad about the pants, and Pop blamed "The Crime Club." I gave Cider his first bath and he liked it. Cider looks pretty doggy tonight with his white feet and white nose. Dropped one of Mom's dishes and was sent to bed early. I'm just as well satisfied, because I'll have plenty of time to think about Jean's party.

SUNDAY, October 30

Pop took the family for a ride through the country. Leaves have turned into a million colors. Cornhusks are piled high in the fields. Guess the summer is gone all right. Bo came over tonight dressed in the costume he will wear at Jean's party. He looked like a colored man from the South — had his face blackened and carried a banjo. Mom and Pop had a big laugh when they saw him. I put on my Indian suit but didn't paint my face. That will come tomorrow night. Bet there'll be more fun at Jean's party than at Virginia Drake's. Why does there have to be school tomorrow? Why can't parties start in the morning and last all day, especially, when they are at Jean Wallace's house? Think I'll start something like that when I become President.

MONDAY, October 31

Just got home from Jean's party. Feel too bad to write anything tonight. Guess all girls are alike!

TUESDAY, November 1

Don't ever want to see Jean Wallace again. What a party! It wasn't my idea of a good time. When I put my hand into the booth for my fortune, somebody smeared it with lard. I think that "somebody" was

Clint Tucker. I'd like to know who pushed my face into the tub of water, when I was ducking for apples. Clint Tucker sat next to Jean at the table. Helen Rogers was my partner. The way Jean talked and laughed with Clint, you'd have thought that Clint was the only one at the party. Doesn't Clint know that Jean is my girl? Well, she's *not* my girl any more. You can't depend on girls. That's why I've put them out of my life. I'll be an unmarried President. I'm through with girls.

WEDNESDAY, November 2

Asked Sister Agnes to change my seat but she refused. I don't want to sit near Jean Wallace. That's what you get for being nice to a girl. I'll never mention Jean Wallace again. After this, she'll be known as "The Spider." For the very, very, very last time of all times, I write "Jean Wallace."

THURSDAY, November 3

Caught the Spider looking at me several times, but buried myself in my books. She dropped her pencil three times and I knew that they weren't accidents. The third time the pencil rolled right under my seat, but I never moved. She tried to signal me, but I was too busy studying the French and Indian Wars. Gee, girls are funny. They certainly chase us boys. You'd think that they'd know that we don't want to be bothered. Suppose girls don't know any better. That's why they're girls — they don't know enough to be boys.

FRIDAY, November 4

Still mad at the Spider and I'm going to stay that way.

SATURDAY, November 5

Cleaned the cellar and sold my newspapers to the ragman for thirty-eight cents. Put a quarter in my bank. Froggie wanted me to go to the movies. Feature picture was "The Spider Crawls." Wouldn't go because I know too much about spiders, especially, One Certain Spider. Went over to Terry's and listened to the football game. Notre Dame beat the Army. Hope I can go to Notre Dame some day.

SUNDAY, November 6

Pumpkin pie today, the first of the season! Froggie, Terry, and I went to the movies to see "Night Riders" and "The Last of the Sea Pirates." Two swell pictures! Mrs. Conway and Ted came over this evening. Mom made coffee and cinnamon toast. Wish the Conways would come often, because I like cinnamon toast. The Spider wore a new hat today, but I didn't look at it.

MONDAY, November 7

Father Foley gave us our reports today. Passed in everything except drawing, which is not so important. Anyway, a President doesn't have to be an artist. Father Foley praised the Spider for her fine report, but I didn't listen. I don't want to hear anything about girls. The Beaver Chiefs borrowed Clint Tucker's porch steps tonight. They ought to help our bonfire on election night.

TUESDAY, November 8

Election day! The democrats won. Had a bonfire in Welch's vacant lot. Someone called the fire department before we could use Clint Tucker's steps. Wouldn't I like to be a fireman on election night! Went pushing doorbells on Grant St. Mr. Rogers chased us and the Beaver Chiefs ran to the four corners of the earth. Anyway, the democrats won, and we did our part to celebrate.

WEDNESDAY, November 9

What a day! Clint Tucker told Father Foley that the Beaver Chiefs stole his porch steps. We tried to tell Father Foley that we only borrowed them. Father Foley said that the Beaver Chiefs had disgraced Holy Cross School and he made us take the steps back. Mrs. Tucker called us criminals. We're not criminals, because we're not old enough to be criminals. Some people can't see any fun in life — meaning Mrs. Tucker.

THURSDAY, November 10

The Spider left a note on my desk. Read the note after school. The Spider said that she was sorry that I got into trouble. She certainly wasn't sorry when she saw me in trouble at her party. Isn't that just like a girl though? Girls are always chasing us boys. Well, the

Spider can chase, and chase, and chase. My mind's made up.

FRIDAY, November 11
Armistice Day! No school! The Beaver Chiefs went to the parade this morning. Pop marched with the Veterans of Foreign Wars. When Pop marched by with his gun on his shoulder, the Beaver Chiefs clapped, and that pleased Pop. After the parade Pop took Froggie, Terry, Bo, and me for a ride. He told us a lot of stories about the war. Imagine having a father who helped make the world safe for the democrats, or something like that. Hope there will be no wars while I am President. I want to enjoy myself.

SATURDAY, November 12
Mom met Mrs. Wallace and the Spider at the market today. Mom thinks that the Spider is beautiful, lovely, and charming. The Spider may be beautiful, lovely, and charming, but why should I care? Girls are out of my life. If I hadn't made up my mind to be President, I'd be a sailor. Then the girls couldn't bother me.

SUNDAY, November 13
Father Foley preached about being kind to your neighbor and not holding grudges. He said that only small people have enemies. That hurt me. Father Foley said that we should mean what we say, when we pray "forgive us our trespasses, as we forgive those who trespass against us." Something inside of me kept

saying: "He means you, Pomp. He means you." After church the Spider said: "Good morning, Pompey." I smiled and said: "Good morning, Jean!" Somehow I felt better right away. Father Foley doesn't know it, but he did a little fixing.

MONDAY, November 14
Jean Wallace gave me some candy today. Mom was right. Jean *is* beautiful, lovely, and charming. What's the use of having enemies, especially, girl enemies? As Father Foley said: "Only small people have enemies." Gave Cider a bath after school. Guess he didn't like it because the water was cold.

TUESDAY, November 15
Holy Cross School is going to have a basketball team. Had our first practice tonight. Father Foley will be our coach. He told us that basketball will develop our characters. We voted to call the team "The Beaver Chiefs." Father Foley promised to buy suits for the team. Those who make the best showing in practice will make the first team. Believe me, I'm going to work hard and land a place on that team. Another practice tomorrow night.

WEDNESDAY, November 16
Jean Wallace told me that she'd pray that I would make the team. That's what I call a friend. School seemed long today. Thought the bell would never ring so that we could get over to the hall for practice.

Father Foley taught us the "five-man defense." I shot two baskets during the practice. Father Foley will pick the team on Friday. Had pancakes for supper and ate eleven of them. Wish I knew what saint is the patron of basketball players. I'd like to ask him to help me make the team.

THURSDAY, November 17

Virginia Drake gave me a new pencil. Jean didn't seem to like it. Bet Virginia won't have any trouble getting married, because she's pretty nice all ready. Think I'll make Virginia my second best girl. Suppose I'll have a million girls, when they find out that I'm going to be President. Practiced again tonight. Made two baskets and shot one foul in the scrub game. Boy, how I'm praying and working to make that team! Clara and Mom have gone to the movies. Dish night again!

FRIDAY, November 18

Sister Agnes had one of her tired days — a test this morning, and another test this afternoon. Oh boy, oh boy, oh boy, *I made the team.* Father Foley said that I could play forward on the first team. Froggie will play center and Terry will be one of the guards. Bo will be one of the substitutes. We were measured for uniforms this afternoon. First game will be Thanksgiving Eve. We will play the Grant St. Terriers. Oh boy, oh boy, oh boy!

SATURDAY, November 19

The Beaver Chiefs practiced for an hour this morning. Could have practiced all day, but Father Foley said that we mustn't burn ourselves out — whatever that means. Of course, Father Foley must know, because he played basketball when he was in college. Mom bought me a pair of basketball shoes this afternoon, and Mom bought Pop a red necktie, which will be mine some day. Went to confession, because I want to keep the Lord on my side. We must beat those Grant St. Terriers. Clara has gone to a dance with Bud Hastings. Going to bed early.

SUNDAY, November 20

Gee, it's funny how hard you can pray when you want something. Told Jesus to be sure and be at the basketball game on Wednesday night, because we'll need Him. Hope the other Chiefs are praying as hard as I am. Pop took me to a clambake this afternoon. There were bushels of sweet potatoes, but I didn't eat any, because I have to keep in condition for the game. Potatoes make you fat. Had plenty of clams and chicken. Whoever started clambakes, certainly knew his business.

MONDAY, November 21

Snowed for five minutes this morning. Nurses came to school today and cleaned our teeth. A nurse told me that I have lovely teeth. I believed her until I found out that she said the same thing to Froggie, and Terry, and Bo. That's the woman of it — always trying to fool us men. Had a long practice tonight and the team looked pretty good. Father Foley gave us a "pep talk" — told us to play clean and to be good sports. He said that the better team is always a good loser, which is something to remember. Hope Father Foley doesn't think that we're going to lose, especially, after all my prayers. Certainly don't want to have my prayers wasted. Am going to bed early, because athletes have to keep in condition.

TUESDAY, November 22

At this time tomorrow night we'll be beating the Grant St. Terriers. Had our final practice. Father Foley gave us some signals which we can't tell to anybody, not even to our best friends. Boy, that makes one feel important! Our suits are honeys — red trunks, white shirts, and across the front of the shirts is written in red letters "Beaver Chiefs." Mom, Pop, and Clara are going to the game, and so are Jean and Mrs. Wallace. Admission will be ten cents. Am going to say some extra prayers to the patron saint of basketball players. Bet I won't sleep a wink.

WEDNESDAY, November 23

The Beaver Chiefs won their first game, and what a game! Hall was packed. Eighth-grade girls formed a cheering section. Crowd clapped when we appeared in our new uniforms. Grant St. Terriers didn't have uniforms. Game ended in a tie with the score 12 to 12. Had to play an extra period. Thought the period would never end. Gannon of the Terriers fouled me and the referee called for strict silence. I said a "Hail Mary" in a hurry and made the basket. The crowd went wild. We managed to hold on to the ball until the whistle blew. Final score was 13 to 12 in our favor. Father Foley shook my hand after the game and said that I was a credit to Holy Cross. Mom invited Mrs. Wallace and Jean to the house and we had sandwiches and coffee. Today, I think, was the best day of my life, and the happiest. The turkey is all stuffed, waiting for tomorrow.

THURSDAY, November 24

Small piece in the paper about the game. It said that last night Pompey Briggs led the Holy Cross Beaver Chiefs to a thrilling victory. Cut out the piece and put it in my prayer book where I can see it often. Certainly had a lot to be thankful for today — our victory, Mom, Pop, Jean, and being president of the Beaver Chiefs. Showed my thanks by eating bushels of the grandest dinner in town — fruit cup, celery, olives, pickles, turkey, and more turkey, and more turkey, sweet potatoes, squash, cider, and mince pie. Guess all athletes swear off on Thanksgiving Day, and I certainly did my part. Pop took us for a ride this afternoon. Came home hungry and ate more turkey. God is a pretty good God to the Briggs family, if you ask me. Jean phoned and said that she saw the piece in the paper.

Virginia Drake phoned too. Looks as though Pomp is a hero.

FRIDAY, November 25

No school today. Helped Mom clean the pantry. Codfish for dinner! What a drop! Pop said that the change was too much and I agreed with him. Whoever discovered codfish did an awful job. Well, I suppose if we had turkey every day, why, after a while, turkey would be nothing more than codfish. There's an idea — turkey-codfish.

SATURDAY, November 26

Landed a job at Conlan's Grocery. Ran some errands and helped at the fruit counter. Mr. Conlan gave me a dollar and said that I could work every Saturday. Oh boy, oh boy, oh boy! Why didn't I think of a job before this time? Mom said that I could keep the money, but I mustn't waste it. Pop said that the man who saves is never sorry, and Pop should know. Think I'll put half a dollar in my bank every week, and when I grow up, I'll have lots of money. Presidents need money, especially, when they go on long vacations, which I certainly am going to do. Bought Cider a rubber ball for a nickel. He played with the ball all evening, even took it to bed with him. Suppose that's his way of saying "thanks."

SUNDAY, November 27

Father Foley read Mom's name in church to help at

the church bazaar. Mom will have charge of the apron booth. She called up all of her friends today, and she has twenty-six donations already. The Beaver Chiefs went for a walk this afternoon. Certainly looks like Christmas uptown. All of the windows are decorated. Mannion's window is the best, with Santa Claus climbing down a chimney with a bag of toys. What I wouldn't give to have a million dollars! Just think of all the things I could buy with that money. Wonder if Presidents ever become millionaires!

MONDAY, November 28

Back to school! Terry Mann has a new red sweater with a zipper front. The Monitors have challenged the Beaver Chiefs. Game will be played on Friday night. Father Foley said that we must win for Holy Cross. We'll show him what the Beaver Chiefs can do. Mom has twelve more donations. Mrs. Conway and Mrs. Drake are helping her. Cider chewed a big hole in his ball, and it is no longer a ball. Looks as though the Beaver Chiefs will never have time for another meeting. Basketball is better than meetings anyway.

TUESDAY, November 29

Started reading *Evangeline* in school today. Can't see why they put a story about a girl in the eighth grade. Why can't all stories be like *Horatio at the Bridge,* and *The Man Without a Country?* If I ever meet this Longfellow, I'll tell him something. Maybe he thinks that *Evangeline* is pretty good stuff, but to me it is trash, and that's what Froggie thinks too. Couldn't practice tonight because Father Foley had to go to a meeting. Mom is getting plenty of aprons.

WEDNESDAY, November 30

The last day of the month! What a month! Lost my girl, then won her back. The Beaver Chiefs won their first game. Thanksgiving. That was a lot to crowd into one month. More *Evangeline* today, and I am sick of her already. The team practiced tonight and we went like a house on fire. Father Foley played with us for a while. You ought to see him drop in those baskets, away from the center of the court. Boy, he's a great priest. He certainly must like the Beaver Chiefs, because he gives us so much of his time. Think I'll say a prayer for Father Foley tonight, even though he doesn't need it.

THURSDAY, December 1

Mom sent a basket of fruit, potatoes, bacon, vegetables, bread, and tea, to poor Mrs. Billings. When I delivered the basket, Mrs. Billings cried, and said that she would pray for Mom tonight. Wish I had a lot of money so that I could be good to the poor. Mom and Clara have gone to the movies for more dishes. They have enough dinner plates, cups, and saucers. Now they're starting on the vegetable dishes.

FRIDAY, December 2

We beat the Monitors. Score was 11 to 6. I scored four

points. In the dressing room Froggie made me mad when he accused me of hogging the ball. Lost my temper, hit Froggie, and knocked him down. Right after I did it, I felt so ashamed that I could have cried, but I didn't. When Froggie left the dressing room, he never said a word. Neither did I. Why is it that you always hurt most the people you like best? Maybe, I'm made wrong.

SATURDAY, December 3
Worked in the store all day. Everybody was buying oranges because we had a sale. Mr. Conlan gave me another dollar for pay. Stopped in Bo's house on the way home. Bo said that Froggie called me a "Prima Donna." Gee, I never expected that from Froggie.

SUNDAY, December 4
Felt bad all day. After church Betty Bauer called me "Mr. Prima Donna." That made me mad. Went over to Bo's house this afternoon but Bo and Froggie were at the movies. Came home and read a book. Took Cider for a walk after supper. Mrs. Drake is downstairs visiting with Mom, but I'm going to bed.

MONDAY, December 5
Received our reports this morning. I failed in history. Pop said that if I paid more attention to the great men of history, and less attention to The Crime Club, meaning, of course, the Beaver Chiefs, I'd be better

off. Have an awful headache tonight, but didn't tell Mom. Was afraid she'd give me castor oil. Ugh!

TUESDAY, December 6
Awful sick today. Didn't go to school.

WEDNESDAY, December 7
Still sick. Head feels like a ball of fire.

THURSDAY, December 8
Doctor Dugan came today. I have the grippe. Swell way to spend a holiday.

FRIDAY, December 9
Doctor Dugan came again. Feel better tonight. Had bread and milk for supper. Doctor said that I could sit up tomorrow.

SATURDAY, December 10
Looks as though Pomp will live to be President. Felt much better today. Sat up all afternoon. Mrs. Wallace brought me some oranges, and Jean gave me a book called *Be Sick and Like It*. Every page has a laugh. Terry and Bo stopped in tonight and said that Froggie is still mad. Mr. Conlan told Mom to tell me not to worry about my job. It was a dandy day, except whenever I thought about Froggie.

SUNDAY, December 11
Boy, was I surprised this morning! Froggie stopped in after church. Gee, I was ashamed when Froggie

shook my hand and said that I was not a "Prima Donna." You know, I never liked Froggie half so much as I have since the fight. Now I feel better than ever. Wouldn't have felt so bad if he didn't belong to the Beaver Chiefs. The good part of being mad at somebody is, that after you make up, you always feel better.

MONDAY, December 12

Went back to school. The class finished *Evangeline* while I was sick, for which I give thanks. Sickness is good for something after all. Jean said that she was glad to see me back. No basketball this week because they are fixing the booths for the bazaar. Mom is still gathering in the aprons. This parish will be full of aprons by next Saturday night.

TUESDAY, December 13

Snowed all day. Terribly cold tonight. Sweet potatoes and apple pie for supper. Sometimes I think Mom is a mind reader. Just when I want sweet potatoes, Mom has them. When I want apple pie, Mom never fails me. Wonder if all mothers are like Mom! I certainly, wouldn't trade mothers with anybody. I'd be afraid to take a chance.

WEDNESDAY, December 14

Froggie's aunt died, the one who always gave him five dollars for Christmas. Poor Froggie, with Christmas only a few days away! Finished our course in history today. Will start to review tomorrow. Pop brought his boss, Mr. Caldwell, home for supper tonight. Even though he is a boss, Mr. Caldwell is a fine man. Mr. Caldwell said that he read about the Beaver Chiefs' basketball team in the paper. Bet that made Pop proud.

THURSDAY, December 15

After school the Beaver Chiefs went uptown. Didn't buy anything, just looked around. Saw a nice tie which I think Pop will like for Christmas. Clara will get handkerchiefs. Couldn't find anything for Mom. Wonder if I ought to buy something for Jean Wallace because she's my girl! The bazaar opened tonight. Clara took Helen Burke to the movies so that Helen could get Mom's dish for her. Hope Mom makes plenty of money for Father Foley. Cider is going to sleep with me because it's a pretty cold night, and dogs get cold, just like boys.

FRIDAY, December 16

Mom made eighty-three dollars on the aprons last night. Had another test in arithmetic. Just when you begin to feel pretty good about the bazaar, and Christmas, and everything, then Sister has to give a test. Believe me, when I become President, I'll pull that word "test" out of the dictionary. I'll make America different from every other country in the world — a country where eighth grades, seventh grades, and all other grades, will never have a test.

SATURDAY, December 17

Worked all day at Conlan's Grocery. After supper Mom, Pop, Clara, Aunt Sarah, and I went to the bazaar. Spent all of my pay but had plenty of fun. Treated Mrs. Wallace and Jean to ice cream. Pop won a blanket and I won a basket of groceries. Tried to win one of Mom's aprons, but couldn't. Felt big spending my own money. Father Foley treated me to Coca-Cola. No wonder everybody likes him. Mom's booth made three hundred and eighteen dollars for the three nights. Mom is very happy tonight. So am I, because I won the groceries.

SUNDAY, December 18

Received Holy Communion this morning. Father Foley announced that they made seventeen hundred and thirty-four dollars on the bazaar. If you ask me, that's a heap of money in anybody's language. Counted the money in my bank and have two dollars and eighty-four cents, which I'm going to spend for Christmas presents. This afternoon Bo and I watched the skaters at Miller's Pond. Just because Clint Tucker can skate backwards, he thinks he's the best skater around these parts. Well, if I had a pair of skates, I'd show him.

MONDAY, December 19

School was great today. Sister Agnes read "The Birds' Christmas Carol." That's my idea of a swell story. Sister promised to read "The Other Wise Man" tomorrow. Well, it will have to be good to beat "The Birds' Christmas Carol." Went uptown alone to buy my Christmas presents. Bought Clara three handkerchiefs for twenty cents. Pop's tie cost thirty-five cents. Paid seventy-five cents for Mom's present. Bought Mom a prayer book which the lady wrapped in tissue paper. Mom wanted to know what the packages were, but I hid them in the bottom drawer of my dresser. Will buy Jean's present tomorrow.

TUESDAY, December 20

"The Other Wise Man" was good, but not as good as "The Birds' Christmas Carol." Went uptown and bought Jean a bottle of Christmas Night in Paris perfume for forty cents. The present is in a white box which is tied with red ribbon. Bet my present will be the best present that Jean will receive. At least, that's what I hope.

WEDNESDAY, December 21

Why can't Christmas come more often? Father Foley gave each one in the class a Rosary. School closed for the holidays, for which I say "thanks, thanks, thanks." Had to go uptown again, because I forgot to buy something for Cider. Bought him a bowl with a dog's picture on the side of it — a bowl for his hamburg and carrots. Christmas shopping is a job, but it's fun when you know that your presents will make people happy. Terry and Froggie came over tonight. Mom treated us to cake and cocoa.

THURSDAY, December 22

Boy, Mom made Christmas cookies today. Took some cookies to Aunt Sarah and she gave me a piece of mince pie. As a rule, aunts are pretty good, especially when they make mince pies. The Beaver Chiefs went tobogganing this afternoon and we had a great time. Tore my pants, but Mom didn't seem to care, because Mom has the Christmas spirit. Mom received a Christmas card from Mrs. Wallace and a calendar from Father Foley. No mail and no presents for Pompey Briggs. Of course, it's early, but just the same, I don't want to be overlooked. That's one thing about believing in Santa Claus. When you believe in Santa Claus, you are always certain that you will get something.

FRIDAY, December 23

Had to work at Conlan's Grocery because of the Christmas rush. Guess everybody in the neighborhood will eat oranges and walnuts. Received a card from Aunt Sarah, addressed to "Master Pompey Briggs." Master! Doesn't Aunt Sarah know that I'm in the eighth grade now, and a workingman besides, and you don't call such people "Master"? Bet the mailman laughed when he read it. Pop bought a tree today and we trimmed it tonight. That old Christmas spirit certainly works miracles, especially with Clara.

SATURDAY, December 24

Mr. Conlan must have made a thousand dollars today, because everybody bought groceries. Am tired but happy. Mr. Conlan gave me an extra dollar, a bag of oranges, and a box of candy. That's what I call a swell boss. Am going to take a nap for a couple of hours. Mom said that she would call me at half-past ten and that I could go to Midnight Mass with her and Pop and Clara. Oh boy, that means that we won't go to bed until tomorrow. Received a card from Virginia Drake, one from Froggie, one from Bo, and one from Terry, but none from Jean Wallace. That's got me wondering.

SUNDAY, December 25

The best day of the year! Midnight Mass was great. Just before Mass began, all the lights went out and the choir sang "Silent Night." Felt as though I was in heaven. After church Jean met me and gave me a dandy muffler. Clara gave me gloves, and best of all, Mom and Pop gave me a pair of skates. Went to bed at two-thirty this morning. Aunt Sarah came for dinner and brought me underwear, the worst present I received. What a dinner of turkey, cranberries, dressing, sweet potatoes, turnips, and mince pie! Thought I'd bust my belt. Took Jean her bottle of Christmas Night in Paris perfume and she liked it. Clint Tucker gave her a gold cross on a chain. Bet he paid five dollars for it. Wonder if he's trying to steal my girl! Suppose I shouldn't think such thoughts on Christmas day! Even though I don't believe in Santa Claus, still he was pretty good to me.

MONDAY, December 26

Cider had his first meal in the new bowl. Guess he liked it all right, because he licked the sides of it. Suppose that's his way of saying "thanks." Froggie, Terry, and I went skating this afternoon. Met Virginia Drake and Jean Wallace at the rink. Skated a lot with Jean and a few times with Virginia. At first, I was nervous skating with girls. Thought everybody was looking at us, and kept praying that I wouldn't fall. Stopped at Jean's house on the way home. Mrs. Wallace treated us to cookies and cocoa. I'll bet that after the Briggs family, the Wallace family is the next best family in Blackford. Pop took the family to the movies tonight. Yes, it was a pretty good day.

TUESDAY, December 27

Pompey Briggs had his eyes opened today. Mom took me uptown this morning and put two dollars in the bank for me. The man gave me a book with my name on it. Mom said that the bank will pay me money for leaving my money there. When I saw the man behind the cage with all that money — my money and hundreds of other people's money — why, then and there I decided that I'm going to be a banker. Boy, it must be great to have thousands of dollars. When I'm a banker, Pop and Mom won't have to work any more. Went skating this afternoon with the Beaver Chiefs. The girls were there too, and so was Clint Tucker. Jean skated mostly with me. Asked Jean to go skating with me alone tomorrow. Jean said that she'd call me tomorrow.

WEDNESDAY, December 28

Girls certainly can't be trusted. Jean called at noon and said that she couldn't go skating because she wasn't feeling well. Bo and I went tobogganing tonight and whom did we meet but Jean Wallace and Clint Tucker! She certainly wasn't very sick, because she seemed to be having the time of her life. Clint took her into the pavilion and bought her hot chocolate. Bo and I had hot chocolate too. Jean called us over to her table, but we wouldn't go. I'll show Jean that she can't lie to me. Clint Tucker can have her, because I'm through with her. Wish I had my Christmas Night in Paris perfume, and I'd give it to Virginia Drake. Jean can have her muffler back too, because I'm not going to wear it.

THURSDAY, December 29

Mom and Clara have gone to the movies. Am mad at the whole world tonight, and especially girls. This afternoon Bo and I met Jean Wallace and Clint Tucker at the skating rink. When I tripped and fell, Jean laughed, and Clint called: "Just an amateur!" That made me mad, and I'm still mad.

FRIDAY, December 30

Went skating with the Beaver Chiefs but didn't see Jean. Skated for a while with Virginia Drake and

Betty Bauer. It was all right, but not as good as it used to be. Cider wasn't feeling well tonight, so Mom and I gave him mineral oil. That always cures him. Clara has a new boy friend, Dick Burroughs. Have to work tomorrow.

SATURDAY, December 31

The last day of the year! Worked in the store all day and we were very busy. Mrs. Wallace and Jean came into the store. Pretended that I was busy. Jean leaned over the counter and said: "Happy New Year, Mr. Briggs!" I just said "thanks," and began shining my apples. I didn't like the way she said "Mister." Mom stuffed another turkey tonight, so it looks like a pretty good beginning for the new year. Am going to try to keep awake, so that I can hear the bells ring at midnight.

SUNDAY, January 1

Fell asleep and didn't hear the bells, but the new year came just the same. Snowed all day. Mom invited Mrs. Conway and Ted for dinner. Ted beat me eating sweet potatoes; he even ate the skins. Made some resolutions, which I now make solemn:

1. To be a good President of the Beaver Chiefs.
2. To save my money and become a banker.
3. To keep on liking sweet potatoes.
4. To become such a good skater that Jean Wallace will beg me to skate with her.

5. Not to be a sissy like Clint Tucker.
6. To be nice to Virginia Drake, even though I am a girl hater.
7. To keep on hating girls.

MONDAY, January 2

Froggie taught me how to skate backwards. When I saw Clint Tucker skating with Jean Wallace, I asked Virginia Drake to skate with me. That's one of my resolutions — to be nice to Virginia. Went over to Terry's house for supper. Boy, can Terry's mother make lemon pie! It was almost as good as Mom's. Wish all days were vacation days!

TUESDAY, January 3

Snowed this morning. Went skating this afternoon. Jean Wallace saw me skating with Virginia Drake and Betty Bauer. Jean told Froggie that she wants to make up with me. Nothing doing, because I made a New Year's resolution to hate girls, and Jean is a girl. I'll never play second place for Clint Tucker. After supper Pop, Mom, Clara, and I went to the movies. It was "Country Store Night" and I won a washtub. Mom said that I'm lucky. I may be lucky when it comes to a washtub, but not so lucky when it comes to a girl.

WEDNESDAY, January 4

Back to school. Jean wore a new blue dress, but I pretended that I didn't see it. Jean looked nicer than ever, but that won't make me break my resolution.

Once I read in a book that women dress just to catch men, and Jean is not going to catch me. No basketball until after the examinations. Reviewed papering and carpeting. It makes me sick when I think of all the things I have to remember just for an exam. Terry gave me a book to read. It's called: "Midnight Murders in a Country Cemetery." Had to sneak it upstairs so that Mom wouldn't see it. Three people murdered already, and I'm only in the fourth chapter. That's what I call a book!

THURSDAY, January 5

Still reviewing, reviewing, reviewing. That old *Evangeline* was trotted out again. Can't understand how *Evangeline* will help a banker. How much good will papering and carpeting do for a banker? Schools are all wrong, if you ask me. The Beaver Chiefs wanted to have a meeting, but there was nothing to meet about, so we went tobogganing. Mom has gone over to visit Mrs. Drake, and I have a date with "Midnight Murders in a Country Cemetery."

FRIDAY, January 6

Father Foley asked me to help him in the library, so I escaped the papering and carpeting. If Father Foley only knew how much I like to work, he certainly would ask me more often. Mom found "Midnight Murders in a Country Cemetery." Mom told Pop, and he made me give the book back to Terry tonight. Anyway, they were good murders while they lasted.

SATURDAY, January 7

Not so busy in the store today, but got my pay just the same. Guess everybody spent their money during the holidays. Put fifty cents in my bank, because that's the way to become a banker. That's what the sign says in the window of the First National Bank: "Teach your pennies to have sense. Save today and have tomorrow." Mrs. Wallace sent Mom a jar of jam, which we had for supper, but I didn't eat any. Catch me eating the jam of the mother of the girl I hate! That would be treason, or something. When Pompey Briggs hates, he doesn't fool around with it, even though he does like jam.

SUNDAY, January 8

The day was made for skating, not too cold, not too warm. Rink was crowded. They had a bonfire at one end of the rink, and a band played all afternoon. The Wallace-Tucker pair tried to show off, but Virginia and I took no back seat. Clint fell and tore his coat, so the lovey-doveys went home early. Walked home with Virginia and carried her skates. Aunt Sarah came for supper, and Pompey Briggs ate candied sweet potatoes, which is one of my New Year's resolutions.

MONDAY, January 9

Back to school! Jean tried to be friendly. Think she wanted to talk to me, but didn't give her the chance. As Napoleon Bonaparte, or George Washington, or maybe it was Longfellow, once said: "Make yourself precious!" That's just what I'm going to do. Mom bought me a new pair of pants, because the old ones were getting pretty thin. Ted Conway's aunt died in New York. Mrs. Conway has gone to the funeral. Ted will sleep with me tonight.

TUESDAY, January 10

Hurrah! Steampipe broke in school. Sister Agnes sent the class home. Ted Conway and I went to Terry Mann's for dinner and had dumplings. Ted will sleep with me again tonight, because Mrs. Conway is still in New York. Hope the pipe won't be fixed tomorrow.

WEDNESDAY, January 11

Pipe fixed! Isn't that always the way things happen? Ted, Froggie, Bo, and I went skating after school. Bo froze his ear and a man rubbed it with snow. Saw Jean Wallace skating with Mart Hanna. Suppose that's a new wrinkle, but isn't that just like a girl? Girls are always changing their minds. Jean can have Mart, because no girl wants him. Mrs. Conway will be home tomorrow, so Ted will sleep with me tonight. Ted is all right except when he steals the blankets while I'm asleep.

THURSDAY, January 12

Had a short test on carpeting and papering. Think I put the carpet on the wall and the paper on the floor. After all, why should bankers bother about such small things? Had fried eggplant for supper and eggplant is on my "no list." Whoever discovered eggplant must have been mad at the whole world. Even Cider refused to eat it, proving that Cider knows something. Dick Burroughs took Clara on a sleigh ride tonight. Some people get all the breaks.

FRIDAY, January 13

Friday, the thirteenth, was certainly an unlucky day. Pop started the day with a flat tire. Helped fix the tire and was late for school. Had to stay after school and write "I was late" four hundred times. Couldn't go skating because of the task. Lost my pocketknife, the one Pop gave me for my birthday. Even Cider fell into trouble. When Mom was upstairs, Cider climbed up on the kitchen table and ate a half pound of butter. Cider couldn't eat any supper tonight, and I don't wonder. Mom and I gave him mineral oil, so Cider must be pretty well greased tonight. Think I'll go to bed before something else happens.

SATURDAY, January 14

Pop took Cider to the doctor this morning. Doctor gave Cider some worm medicine. Can't figure out how butter would make a dog have worms. A dandy day for skating, but had to work in the store all day. Mr. Conlan treated me to cider and doughnuts, which shows that he likes me. Cider is better tonight and we're all happy. Wish I didn't have to take a bath, because it's so cold. Wonder who started this taking baths on Saturday night! Mom said that bankers take baths every day, which won't be so nice. But watch Pompey Briggs do some cheating! Nobody will ever know the difference.

SUNDAY, January 15

Started the day right by receiving Holy Communion. After dinner Froggie, Terry, and I went skating. Jean Wallace was skating with Mart Hanna. Pompey Briggs kept his head high in the air every time he passed them. Virginia Drake didn't show up, so I skated with a girl named Milly. Bet Jean didn't like that. I'll show Jean that I can have any girl I want, and I don't have to want Jean Wallace. Caught Dick Burroughs kissing Clara in the parlor tonight. Dick gave me a quarter and told me to keep quiet, which I will do any day for a quarter. Imagine Clara being kissed by Dick Burroughs! Maybe they call it "love," but I call it "mush."

MONDAY, January 16

Examinations! Tried history and spelling today. Spelling was easy, but the history was too long. Ate half of my pencil trying to figure out a remote cause of the French and Indian War. On the way home stopped to get weighed. Tipped the scale at 118 pounds. A card came out of the slot and told my fortune. It read: "Your life will be a path of roses. You shall have many loves and few disappointments. You shall marry young, and your blond wife will be a great help to you. Your career in the business world will be the envy of your many friends. The future has many things in store for you, but you will have to fight hard for them." Pompey Briggs fights for fame and fortune! Boy, that sounds like Napoleon.

TUESDAY, January 17
Had exams in silent reading and arithmetic. After all that carpeting and papering, there were no questions about them. Had one question on interest, and, of course, we bankers know our interest. The Grant St. Terriers built a snow fort, and the Beaver Chiefs attacked them on the way home from school. The Beaver Chiefs lost and had to retreat in disgrace. If Pop finds out, he'll declare me the leading candidate to succeed Jessie James or Captain Kidd. My getting into trouble always gives Pop a chance to make a speech.

WEDNESDAY, January 18
English exam today. Two questions about *Evangeline* made me sick. Did a great job on the composition, "My Ambition." Now Sister Agnes will know that I'm going to be a banker. After school Jean asked me if I were going her way. I said "No," because I still hate girls. Father Foley has a game with the "Charging Pirates" for a week from Friday. Terry, Bo, and I went over to the rink tonight, but there was no skat-

ing. Stopped in Larkin's Hall to watch the men bowl, but the boss said: "No kids allowed." Beaver Chiefs and in the eighth grade, and he called us "Kids"!

THURSDAY, January 19

Much colder today. Thought school would never end. Boy, it seemed good to practice again. Father Foley wants us to beat the "Charging Pirates," because they've never lost a game. Had hamburg and sweet potatoes for supper tonight. Wonder if they have sweet potatoes in heaven! Father Foley once said that we'll find everything in heaven that will make us happy, and I need sweet potatoes to make me happy. Guess the Lord will take care of that all right.

FRIDAY, January 20

No news from the exams. Sister Agnes said that we'll have our reports next Monday. Had signal practice tonight and Father Foley gave us two new signals. Jean Wallace, Nancy Bauer, and Betty Bauer came over to watch us practice. Just like girls — always following the boys!

SATURDAY, January 21

Dandy day for skating but had to work in the store. Mr. Conlan was not feeling well, so I worked extra hard. Mrs. Drake bought some oranges, and I picked out large ones, because Virginia is my girl. Why can't all girls be nice like Virginia? Clara bought a new rubber ball for Cider. Clara has been trying to keep on my good side ever since I caught Dick Burroughs kissing her.

SUNDAY, January 22

Snowed all day. Went skating this afternoon with Frank Somers. On the way home Frank dared me to smoke a cigarette. Father Foley was driving down Payne St., and he saw me. If Father Foley ever tells Mom, I'll be ruined. Boy, was I sick when I got home! My head was hot and I couldn't eat much supper. Mom looked suspicious but said nothing. Feel as though I have two heads, so I'm going to bed.

MONDAY, January 23

Father Foley gave us our reports. Just when I was beginning to feel happy because I passed with an average of 86, and thinking that nothing would be said about my cigarette smoking, Father Foley called me into the hall. Father Foley said everything that I didn't like to hear, that I had given bad example, that I had disgraced Holy Cross School, and that I was a poor President of the Beaver Chiefs. Worst of all, he suspended me from the basketball team for two weeks. That means that I won't play against the "Charging Pirates." The team practiced tonight but I took a walk. Bo came over after supper and wanted to know why I didn't practice. Told him I was sick, and I am.

TUESDAY, January 24

Everybody seemed to be looking daggers at me today.

You'd think that I was a criminal, just because I smoked a cigarette. Well, all bankers smoke, and I have to be like the rest of them. The Beaver Chiefs practiced again, and I had to take another walk. Almost choked at table tonight, when Mom said that she had invited Aunt Sarah to go with her to the game on Friday night. I must get sick, and I must do it quickly.

WEDNESDAY, January 25

The whole school knows that I've been suspended. Wish that I could get the grippe or something. Just why did Father Foley have to drive down Payne St. when I was smoking that cigarette? Bet I'll never smoke again!

THURSDAY, January 26

Mrs. Bauer told Mom that I had been suspended from the team. Mom took away my skates, and Pop stormed at the supper table. Clara tried to make things worse, and I told Pop that Dick Burroughs kissed her. Then things really blew up. Pop forgot about me and turned on Clara. Was sent to my room at seven o'clock. I'm off the team and everybody is against me. Now I know how people become criminals. Pompey Briggs, World's Greatest Criminal!

FRIDAY, January 27

Had to write a composition in English class. My subject was "Crime Pays — By One Who Knows." Tonight was the night of the game with the "Charging Pirates." Pop made me go to the game for punishment. Had to pay to see the game. The Chiefs beat the "Charging Pirates," but somehow, I wasn't so happy. It was awful to have to sit through that game, when I should have been playing. This house is just like a morgue, so I'm going to bed.

SATURDAY, January 28
Worked in the store, but didn't have much pep. Mr. Conlan spoke to me about being suspended, and that made me feel bad. Supper was a very quiet affair — no talking, no joking. Guess I'm the family criminal, all right. Clara won't even look at me. With so many girls in this world, why did I have to get Clara for a sister?

SUNDAY, January 29
Went to early Mass, so I wouldn't have to meet so many people. Made up my mind to see Father Foley today. After dinner I went to Father Foley's house. Was so nervous that my knees shook. Promised Father Foley that I'd never smoke again, and asked him to forgive me. Father Foley shook my hand and told me to forget it. Was so happy that I cried. Father Foley put me back on the team and said that I could play Friday against the "Eagles." Father Foley walked home with me, and told the good news to Mom and Pop, and that made them happy. Once more our house is home, sweet home. Pompey Briggs is living again

and goes to bed tonight with a clean conscience. It was certainly an awful week.

MONDAY, January 30

Everybody knows that I am back on the team. Jean Wallace was the first one to shake my hand. I was so happy that I forgot that I was hating her. The team practiced tonight, and boy, it seemed good. Mom gave my skates back. After supper Terry and I went for a walk. Guess I'll go to bed early. Why do people always go to bed when they're awake, and get up when they're asleep? I wonder!

TUESDAY, January 31

Sister Agnes was sick today, so we had a substitute. She can't be much of a teacher, because she gave us a test this morning and another one this afternoon. Cider was sick tonight, so we gave him more medicine. Mom took Clara and me to the movies. As we passed Moulson's Drugstore, I saw Jean Wallace with Clint Tucker. Can you beat that? Kept thinking about them during the show, and didn't enjoy the picture. Clint's always hanging around girls. Wish Jean Wallace would get some brains and stop liking him.

WEDNESDAY, February 1

Sister Rose is the substitute teacher. She didn't have nerve enough to give us more tests, so she taught things that we learned in the seventh grade. Had a long practice tonight. Dick Burroughs came for supper and gave me some dirty looks. After supper I went into the parlor, read the paper, and spoiled Dick's chance of kissing Clara again. After Mom finished the dishes, I went tobogganing with Bo. Didn't see anybody that we didn't want to see — meaning a certain daughter of Mrs. Wallace.

THURSDAY, February 2

Sister Agnes was back today, crosser than ever. You'd think that after having a vacation, she'd find it easy to smile. Why do they always pick teachers who can't smile? I must look that up some time. Had our last practice before the game with the "Eagles." Believe me, I'll play my head off tomorrow night, because Pop, Mom, Aunt Sarah, Dick Burroughs, and Clara will be at the game. I'll make up for last week. After supper the Beaver Chiefs went skating. Jean was skating with Mart Hanna. Wonder if all girls cheat like that — pretend to one fellow that he is grand, and then when he isn't looking, go with someone else! Seems as though girls can do anything and get away with it. I smoked one cigarette and fell into a mess of trouble. My room is cold, so I'm going to bed.

FRIDAY, February 3

Hall was crowded for the game with the "Eagles." We lost to a better team by a score of 10 to 7. With three minutes to play, Terry Mann fell and broke his arm. Father Foley, Pop, and I took Terry to the hospital. Doctor set Terry's arm and Terry will have to stay in the hospital all night. His arm will be in a cast for several weeks. Father Foley feels bad, and so do the Beaver Chiefs, especially the President. Terry didn't deserve it.

SATURDAY, February 4

After work Pop and I went to the hospital and brought Terry home. Terry has no pain, but the cast makes his arm feel like a ton of bricks. Terry let me write my name on the cast. Just as we were leaving Terry's house, we met Mrs. Wallace and Jean. Had to say "Good Evening," because Pomp is a gentleman.

SUNDAY, February 5

Offered my Communion for Terry and asked God to hurry things along. Mom invited Terry for dinner. Jean's name is written on the cast, right under my name. Pop had to carve Terry's meat and we had lots of fun. After dinner Terry and I went to see "The Mystery of the Floating Island" and "The Return of Captain Blake." Two swell pictures! Clara went on a sleigh ride with Dick Burroughs.

MONDAY, February 6

Terry came to school but couldn't write. That's what I call luck. Norm Carter will take Terry's place on the team, until Terry is able to play again. Father Foley has a game with the "Silver Streaks" for Friday night. No practice tonight, because Father Foley had to go to a meeting. Bo and I went tobogganing. On the way home we decided to take up a collection and give Terry a present at the game on Friday. Bo promised to give a quarter. I'll give fifty cents. Boy, won't Terry be surprised? Mom took some of my money to the bank today. Pompey Briggs now has six dollars in the First National Bank. It won't be long before they'll be writing my name over the door.

TUESDAY, February 7

Spread the news about the present for Terry and everybody thought it a great idea. Father Foley gave us a dollar, and the others will bring their money tomorrow. Received an invitation to a Valentine party from Virginia Drake. Bet it will be a better party than the Halloween party, because Virginia is a lady. When I hate girls, I never mean Virginia, because she's too nice to hate. Mom had steak and sweet potatoes for supper. Boy, they were good, especially, the sweet potatoes. Broke one of Mom's dishes, but Mom didn't care, because it was a dish from the dime store.

WEDNESDAY, February 8

Boy, how the money rolled in for Terry's present! We have eight dollars and thirty-five cents. Feel like a real banker, because I'm holding the money. Mom, Mrs. Drake, and Mrs. Carter will buy the present tomorrow. The team had a good workout tonight. I feel it in my bones that we will trim the "Silver Streaks." Last night somebody broke into the garage and stole one of Pop's tires and a chest of tools. Pop called the police, and they promised to work hard to catch the thief.

THURSDAY, February 9

Mom, Mrs. Drake, and Mrs. Carter bought Terry a windbreaker. It cost nine dollars and the ladies made up the balance. Bo, Froggie, and Norm Carter were over tonight, and all said that Terry is worth it. Never had so much fun. It makes you feel like Christmas. Tomorrow will be some night. No news about Pop's tire or the tool chest.

FRIDAY, February 10

Had the largest crowd of the season for our game with the "Silver Streaks." The Beaver Chiefs won. Score was 15 to 11. Father Foley made a speech and gave the windbreaker to Terry. Terry had the surprise of his life. The crowd yelled for Terry to make a speech. Terry tried, but was so happy that he cried. I almost cried myself. What makes people cry when they're happy? And boy, I'm happy tonight. After the game Jean Wallace told me that she was proud of me, because I had been so good to Terry. Somehow, I don't seem to hate Jean so much tonight. Maybe, I'm becoming a sissy.

SATURDAY, February 11

Decided to take a bath before supper. While the water was running into the tub, I lay on the bed to read the funnies. Forgot about the water and the tub overflowed. Some water went through the floor and spoiled the dining-room ceiling. Pop stormed and raved and said that I am careless and shiftless. Eating supper was like having a picnic in a morgue. If I were a banker now, I could have the dining-room papered, and home would be home. Am going to bed early and drown my sorrow.

SUNDAY, February 12
Mom and Pop are still talking about their careless, shiftless son. Heard Pop tell Mom that I'm a bad boy. "Yes," answered Mom, "but don't forget, Pomp is a good bad boy." Now that's something. *Pompey Briggs, the good bad boy!*

MONDAY, February 13
The police found Pop's tire and the chest of tools. Three men were arrested for stealing, and the police found the tire and tools in one of their cellars. Pop and Mom are so happy tonight that they've forgotten the spoiled ceiling. Mom said that stealing doesn't pay. I agree with Mom.

TUESDAY, February 14
Valentine Day! Just came from Virginia's party. Boy, oh boy, that was a party. Bo won the peanut hunt and received a knife for a prize. What a lunch! Sandwiches, potato salad, beans, coffee, ice cream, and cake with red hearts on the frosting. Jean Wallace looked just as my best girl should look in her new red dress.

Walked home with Jean. She gave me an envelope, which I just opened. On a red heart Jean had written the following in white ink:

> Perhaps you think I love someone else.
> If you do, it isn't true.
> I give my heart to the one I love,
> And that one, Pompey, is you.

Looks as though I now have two girls, and two girls are one too many.

WEDNESDAY, February 15

Sister Agnes announced that we shall begin to study algebra next week. Can't figure how we can study arithmetic without numbers, and that's what they call algebra. Terry wore the new windbreaker today and he looked swell. Terry's arm looks like an autograph book with all our names written on the cast. After school Bo and I went skating with Jean and Virginia. Thanked Jean for the Valentine and she blushed. Tried to tell her that I feel the same way she does, but didn't know how to say it. Maybe, she understands. I've often heard Pop say that women know everything.

THURSDAY, February 16

After school the Beaver Chiefs had a meeting. Nobody paid any dues. We decided to have a skating party on Sunday afternoon. Each of the Chiefs must ask a girl.

Just my luck to have two girls on my hands! Think I'll ask Jean and figure out something for Virginia later. Maybe, I can get Froggie to ask Virginia, then, when I ask Virginia, she'll have accepted Froggie's invitation. It will be a great plan if it works.

FRIDAY, February 17
Invited Jean to the skating party and she accepted. Froggie said that he would ask Virginia this noon. Froggie forgot to ask Virginia, and when I asked her tonight, she said she'd be glad to go. I almost fainted, because I was sure that she'd say "No." That's what I get for not playing square. Hope it pours rain Sunday. Hope it gets so warm that we will have to put up the fly screens. Something big must happen to get me out of this kettle of fish. Father Foley took the Beaver Chiefs to the hockey game tonight. Boy, how those fellows could skate! Whenever I think about the skating party, I get sick. Tonight's paper said, "colder weather tomorrow and continued cold for Sunday." It would.

SATURDAY, February 18
Found it hard to work today. Every time a girl came into the store, I saw double. Mr. Conlan knew that something was wrong, because he asked me if I were sick. If Mr. Conlan only knew what was going on inside of me, he would have known that I was very sick. Froggie feels bad, but I can't blame him. Guess my heart needs a zipper. Suppose I have it coming to me.

Mom always says that if you don't play square, you'll pay the price. Guess Mom is right.

SUNDAY, February 19
Prayed my head off in church that something would happen. They must have been pretty good prayers, because they worked. Jean phoned at noon and said that her aunt and uncle had come from Newark. She was sorry that she couldn't go to the skating party. Pretended I was sorry, too. Went skating with Virginia but didn't have much fun. Don't feel just right tonight. Pompey Briggs has been a cheater, and nobody likes cheaters.

MONDAY, February 20
Started the algebra today. Instead of x, or y, or z, why don't they use numbers and be done with it! Just goes to show that people who run schools are not so smart. Imagine buying x worth of beans, or a dozen of oranges for z! Well, I hope Mr. Conlan never pays my wages in x, y, or z. I'll stick to the good old money of George Washington, or Benjamin Franklin, or whoever invented money. Why change things when everything is going along all right?

TUESDAY, February 21
Father Foley has a game with the "Indian Rebels" for Friday night. Had a long practice after school. After supper Pop and I started to take the paper off the walls of the dining room. Right in the middle of

things Mrs. Drake and Virginia called, and we had to stop working. Felt ashamed every time I looked at Virginia and thought of the skating party. It's a good thing that people don't know your thoughts.

WEDNESDAY, February 22

First day of Lent. Think I'll fast from candy. Why did George Washington have to be born today? Today was a holiday, but Mom made me work in the dining room. The Beaver Chiefs went tobogganing this morning, and skating this afternoon, but the President of the Beaver Chiefs worked in the dining room. Bet if Washington knew how I spent his birthday, he'd do something about it.

THURSDAY, February 23

Had to write a composition on "How I Spent Washington's Birthday." Well, I told the truth. Here's what I wrote:

"How I Spent Washington's Birthday"

"I spent Washington's Birthday removing paper from the dining-room walls."

FRIDAY, February 24

Had to stay after school. Sister Agnes wanted me to explain my composition, "How I Spent Washington's Birthday." She laughed when I told her about working in the dining room, and said that she was glad that I'm honest. The paper hangers began work on the dining room today. We beat the "Indian Rebels" by a score of 11 to 6.

SATURDAY, February 25
Pompey Briggs is going to be a policeman. Here's how I figure. Whenever Mr. Nolan, the policeman, comes into Conlan's store, he helps himself to anything he wants. That set me thinking. . . . If a policeman can have anything he sees, then, that's the job for me. Policemen go to ball games and they never pay. Policemen never pay to go to the movies. Well, that's just what I want. Imagine everybody being nice to you! Then, too, policemen don't worry about papering, or carpeting, or x, y, z. What a life! That's the life for Pompey Briggs!

SUNDAY, February 26
Ate in the kitchen today because the dining room isn't finished. Froggie, Bo, and I went to the movies. When I'm a policeman, I'll be going to the movies often. If Father Foley knew that we went to the movies during Lent, we'd hear plenty.

MONDAY, February 27
Mr. Alexander died this morning. Mom spent most of the day with Mrs. Alexander. After school I shoveled her walks and carried up some coal. Mr. Alexander was a good man — always had a smile. Good people

like Mr. Alexander must go straight to heaven. God certainly can't have anything against Mr. Alexander. Nobody else did.

TUESDAY, February 28

The dining room is finished. Mom spent the whole day at Alexander's and Clara did the cooking. Pop and I are going to sit up all night and watch Mr. Alexander, while Mrs. Alexander gets some sleep. First time I ever went to a "wake." Hope I'll like it.

WEDNESDAY, March 1

No more "wakes" for me! After everybody went to bed, Pop and I had a lunch. I liked that part of the "wake," but I didn't like it when Pop fell asleep, and I was left alone with Mr. Alexander. Never heard such quiet stillness in all my life. Thought about the ghost stories I've read and wished that I hadn't read them. The wind blew the door open, and I yelled so loud that Pop woke up. Mrs. Alexander and her sister came running down the stairs in their nightgowns. Then Pop sent me home. Can't understand why dead people have to be watched. Anyway, I'm cured.

THURSDAY, March 2

Two below zero today. Practiced for our game with the "Roving Ramblers." Dick Burroughs came for supper because today was Clara's seventeenth birthday. Am going to bed where it's warm.

FRIDAY, March 3

Algebra test today. Suppose Sister Agnes was tired and we had to suffer. Well, she'll be very tired when she finishes correcting my paper. The Beaver Chiefs are in disgrace. Lost to the "Roving Ramblers" by a score of 14 to 3. They played rings around us. Father Foley said that we'll win the next time. I hope he's right.

SATURDAY, March 4

Feel pretty good tonight, because I just came from confession. Boy, it's great to know that, if you are sorry, God will always forgive you. I hope God understands that, when I do wrong, I don't mean to hurt Him. Anyway, that's what I told Him tonight. Can't see why some people are afraid to go to confession. I always figure that God saw me when I did wrong, so He knows my sins before I tell him. When I tell my sins to Father Foley, I just forget that he's Father Foley. After all, Father Foley just takes God's place. Bet the devil is mad at Pompey Briggs tonight, but I don't care. God is on my side, and the devil can't lick God.

SUNDAY, March 5

Received Communion at the nine o'clock Mass. After dinner I went skating with Jean Wallace. Clint Tucker asked Jean to skate with him, and she left me. Clint even took her home. Wonder if Jean really meant what she said on her Valentine! Pop always says to never trust a woman. I'm beginning to think that Pop is right. Anyway, I still have Virginia Drake.

MONDAY, March 6

Received our reports this morning. Mine was fair with an average of 83. Received 79 in algebra, but that's not worrying me. Have decided not to learn too much algebra, because policemen don't need algebra. Terry went to the doctor today, and the cast is still on his arm. The Beaver Chiefs will try to get back their good name on Friday when they stack up against the "Demons." Had practice tonight. Mom loaned our rattrap to Mrs. Conway, because the rats have been eating Mrs. Conway's flour and apples.

TUESDAY, March 7

During singing class Froggie sang off key. Sister Agnes tried to catch him, but every time she walked near Froggie, he would sing with the rest of us. Believe me, Froggie will never make money as a singer. He sings bad too well. After school the Beaver Chiefs went over to Conway's cellar, and there in our wire trap was a rat. Mrs. Conway was afraid. We wrapped a paper around the trap, and stood on the corner of Payne and Lexington St. A truck came along and had to stop for the lights. We put the trap inside the truck, and the driver never saw us. So Mr. Rat went for a long ride. That was the best way to punish him for eating Mrs. Conway's flour and apples. Wonder how the driver felt when he found that he had a passenger!

WEDNESDAY, March 8

Guess we caught the wrong rat. Ted Conway said that more flour and apples were eaten last night. The Beaver Chiefs fixed another trap with plenty of cheese. Jean Wallace phoned tonight and asked me to take her skating. I made myself important and said that I was busy. Told her to call Clint Tucker or Mart Hanna, and she hung up in a hurry. Bet she called them before she called me. I'm wise to these girls.

THURSDAY, March 9

Sister Agnes caught Froggie changing his voice and made him sing a solo before the whole class. Boy, it was funny. Even though Froggie is a member of the Beaver Chiefs, I had to laugh. Caught another rat in Conway's cellar and we brought him over to our garage. Just getting ready to drown the rat when Pop came along, and he finished the job. Had pigs' hocks and sauerkraut for supper. Mom said that she's going on a diet tomorrow. Mom always says that after a big meal.

FRIDAY, March 10

Mom started the diet this morning with oranges and black coffee for breakfast. She finished the diet tonight. Guess the smell of codfish, baked potatoes, and chocolate pie was too much for her. Mom is just like a certain girl I know — always changing her mind. Rat business was poor today. No catches! Maybe the rats are wise. The "Demons" didn't show up for the game, so we won by a forfeit. Guess they were afraid of us. Father Foley gave the people their money back, and we had to come home early.

SATURDAY, March 11

Had a long talk with Mr. Nolan, the policeman. Mr. Nolan said that policemen have to pass examinations. That's bad, because I don't like examinations. Mrs. Drake was in the store, and said that Virginia has a cold. Gave her some oranges for Virginia, and told Mr. Conlan to take the money out of my pay. Stopped at Ted's house on the way home, and the rat business is poor.

SUNDAY, March 12

Went skating after dinner. Met Jean and skated with her all afternoon. Jean told me not to worry about Clint Tucker or Mart Hanna. She said that she liked them, but I was her best fellow. That made me feel pretty good. Stopped at Jean's house on the way home and she treated me to chocolate fudge. Didn't want to break my Lenten resolution, and didn't want to hurt the feelings of my best girl. Anyway, I took some. Hope God will understand.

MONDAY, March 13

Virginia Drake is sick in bed with a cold. Father Foley announced an Oratory Contest for the eighth-grade boys. Contest will be held one week from tomorrow night. First prize will be ten dollars, second prize will be five dollars, and third prize will be a camera. Clint Tucker told everybody that he'll win first prize. Believe me, I'll try anything for ten dollars, and Clint Tucker will have to be some orator to beat me. Clara said that she will ask Dick Burroughs to help me. No rats in Conway's trap.

TUESDAY, March 14

Father Foley announced that there will be no basketball game on Friday night. He thinks that the Beaver Chiefs need a rest. Mom went to see Virginia Drake this afternoon and brought her some homemade soup. What a thing to bring to a sick person, especially, when the sick person is Virginia Drake! Rat business is still poor, with no customers in the Conway cellar.

WEDNESDAY, March 15

Have decided to give "The Lamp of Life," by Henry Burton, at the Oratory Contest. It is a short poem of three verses. If I win, it will be ten dollars easily earned. If I lose, I won't lose too much. Memorized two verses tonight. Saw Virginia Drake sitting at the window. Looks as though the skating is about through, because it was very warm today. Bought Cider a red ball in the dime store. It took him about five minutes to chew a hole in the ball, so he can go to bed tonight with a clean conscience. Rat business is very, very poor.

THURSDAY, March 16

Went to the doctor's with Terry and his mother. The doctor took the cast off Terry's arm. Terry and I kept pieces of the cast for souvenirs. Terry looks like Terry again. Mom invited him for supper. Had liver, bacon, and sweet potatoes — in other words, it was a real celebration. Know all of my poem for the contest. Believe me, I'm going to work my head off, because I want that ten dollars.

FRIDAY, March 17

Jean Wallace wore a green scarf today in honor of St. Patrick. She invited the Beaver Chiefs to her house tonight for a party. Clint Tucker wasn't there, because he doesn't belong to the Beaver Chiefs. Mrs. Wallace sent some green ice cream to Virginia Drake. Bet Virginia thinks that Mrs. Wallace is the best Mrs. Wallace in the world. That's what I think. Had plenty of fun throwing snowballs on the way home from the party. A policeman chased us, but he slipped and fell in front of Searle's Market. Boy, could that policeman swear!

SATURDAY, March 18

Mr. Conlan raised my pay. Gave me a dollar and a quarter. Think I'll celebrate and take a bath.

SUNDAY, March 19

Rained all day. Had to stay in the house and practice

for the contest. When Dick Burroughs called, I had to practice some more. It's a good thing that policemen don't have to learn poetry. I'll bet that most of the policemen in Blackford sat in movie theaters today, while I recited poetry.

MONDAY, March 20

Virginia Drake returned to school today. Looks as though Sister Agnes wants us to be algebra experts: it's algebra, algebra, algebra. Felt like telling her that she is wasting her time, because I never intend to use it. Good old arithmetic will take care of me, especially, when it comes to counting money. Mom put five dollars in the bank for me. Rat business picked up today. Caught a dandy rat in Conway's cellar and sent him on a long ride. A car with a Jersey license was parked in front of Clayton's house. We put the trap containing Mr. Rat on the floor of the back seat. A lady came out of Clayton's, sat in the front seat and drove away. Boy, will she be surprised, and will she yell! And won't Mr. Rat be mad when he finds himself in Jersey! Mrs. Conway should be mighty thankful to the Beaver Chiefs for doing a good job.

TUESDAY, March 21

Another big day in the life of Pompey Briggs! Hall was crowded for the Oratory Contest. Mom, Pop, Aunt Sarah, Clara, Dick Burroughs, Mrs. Wallace, and Jean sat together. I was so nervous that I never heard a word that the other fellows spoke. Just kept saying my poem over and over, so that I wouldn't forget it. When my turn came, I looked at Father Foley and his smile seemed to help me. My shirt was wringing wet when I finished. Terry Mann won the ten dollars. Pompey Briggs won the five dollars. Mart Hanna won the camera, and Clint Tucker won nothing. As we were leaving the hall, Jean Wallace squeezed my hand and said: "Pomp, I knew you'd do it." For once in their lives, Mom and Pop are proud of me. Suppose they're proud of the good part of their good bad boy.

WEDNESDAY, March 22
Jean Wallace handed me this note this afternoon:

Dear Pompey:

I want you to know how pleased I am that you won second prize last night. When your name was read out, the one who clapped most was

Your sincere friend,

Jean Wallace

That's something worth knowing.

THURSDAY, March 23
Hardly any snow left. Looks as though I'll have to hang up my skates. Bijou, the clown, visited school today. Bijou told us that we should drink lots of milk. He did all kinds of tricks — back flips, walking on his hands, and many others. Bijou said that milk makes one big and strong. Policemen have to be big and

strong, so I'm going to drink milk. Drank my first glass at supper tonight.

FRIDAY, March 24

Ted Conway said that the rats were back last night. Wonder if that rat came back from Jersey! Mrs. Drake let us take her trap, because she doesn't have rats. Made a big feast for Mr. Rat — an apple, a piece of cake, and some cheese. If that isn't a pretty good meal for a rat, I have another guess coming. Drank two glasses of milk today.

SATURDAY, March 25

Mrs. Clement came into the store to buy some rat poison. Being an honest clerk, I told her that rat poison would make the rats die in her cellar. That would be bad. Told her that I knew a firm that would get rid of her rats for a dime a rat. Mrs. Clement said that she would give the firm a trial. So there has been born The Beaver Chief Rat Destroying Company, Incorporated. I'm going to make myself president, because it was my idea. Can't wait until I see the Chiefs tomorrow. Drank one glass of milk.

SUNDAY, March 26

After church the Beaver Chiefs went to Conway's cellar, but there was no rat in the trap. We decided to leave the trap there until tomorrow. The Chiefs felt that a large company, such as ours, shouldn't begin work in the Clement cellar on Sunday. Froggie, Bo, and

I decided to go to the movies this afternoon, but Father Foley changed our minds. Just as we neared the "Lyric," we met Father Foley and he wanted to know where we were going. We pretended that we were going for a walk. Father Foley made us get into his car and he took us for a ride. It seems as though every time we try to put something over, we always get caught.

MONDAY, March 27
The Beaver Chiefs will play the "Merry Madmen" for the championship of the city. The champions will have to win two games out of three. First game will be Friday night. Had a short practice after school. No rats in the Conway cellar. Moved the trap to Mrs. Clement's cellar. Baited the trap with cheese, flour, and an apple. If those rats don't show up, things will be bad for The Beaver Chief Rat Destroying Company, Incorporated. One glass of milk today.

TUESDAY, March 28
Bo and I stopped at Mrs. Clement's this noon, but our bait hadn't been touched. Wouldn't you think that Mrs. Clement's rats would like a good meal? Mrs. Clement seemed disappointed, when we told her that business was poor. Wonder if she expected us to get rid of her rats in one night! Women are like that, you know. Sister Agnes made Jean Wallace read her composition for Father Foley. Sister gave Jean a medal and Jean gave the medal to me. Looks as though I'm

still "number one man" with Jean. Had a long practice tonight. Terry appeared in uniform for the first time since he broke his arm. One glass of milk.

WEDNESDAY, March 29

Mrs. Clement's trap is still empty. Just when we have a chance to make some money, the rats hold a meeting and decide to keep away from our trap. Mom started on the diet again. She did pretty well, until we told her how good her chocolate cake was, and then, she decided to try one piece. That one piece was as big as two pieces for me. Am still drinking milk. Spent the evening at Froggie's house, because Clara's sorority was meeting at our house.

THURSDAY, March 30

Sister Agnes was tired today, so we had an algebra test. She must have been very tired, because all during the test she kept saying: "Take your time, take your time!" She doesn't know it, but I'm wise to her. Had our last practice for the game tomorrow night. Father Foley promised us a party, if we win the championship, and we're going to do just that. Things look bad for The Beaver Chief Rat Destroying Company, Incorporated. It's strange how well things went at the Conway cellar, and the Clement cellar isn't any different. Maybe, Mrs. Clement's rats are too smart.

FRIDAY, March 31

What a day! Lost our first game to the "Merry Madmen." Score was 14 to 9. Father Foley feels very blue tonight, and so do the Beaver Chiefs. Mrs. Clement chased us from her cellar, because we didn't catch any rats. Looks as though The Beaver Chief Rat Destroying Company, Incorporated, will have to uncorporate. Mr. Conlan phoned and told Clara to tell me to come to work tomorrow at eleven o'clock. Believe me, I'm going to enjoy a good long sleep. Mr. Conlan must know that boys like to sleep.

SATURDAY, April 1

Slept until ten o'clock. Mr. Conlan phoned and told me to hurry to work if I wanted to keep my job. When I reached the store, Mr. Conlan was mad. I asked him why he called last night and a smile came over his face. "Pomp," he said, "somebody must have played an April fool joke." I was mad all day. I'll bet Clint Tucker knows something about that phone call. It will be too bad for him, if he does. Mrs. Clement came into the store. She bought rat poison.

SUNDAY, April 2

Palm Sunday! Very warm today. Mom went off the diet again, and I drank a pint of milk. Have decided to say the Rosary each day during Holy Week.

MONDAY, April 3

Pop had a flat tire this morning and was late for work. No basketball during Holy Week. Said my Rosary in church this afternoon. Hope my guardian angel had his eyes open.

87

TUESDAY, April 4

Mrs. Wallace and Jean are going to New York for the Easter vacation. Hope they don't stay too long. Mom had to move the buttons on my pants, because the milk is making me fat. Bijou was right — milk certainly makes one big and strong.

WEDNESDAY, April 5

Easter vacation began at three o'clock. Mrs. Wallace and Jean left for New York tonight. Mom, Clara, and I went to the station. Jean seemed to be very happy, but I felt like crying. That's a girl for you — no heart. All girls are alike.

THURSDAY, April 6

Holy Thursday! The eighth-grade boys formed a guard of honor before the Blessed Sacrament. Ted Conway, Terry, Bo, and I were guards from five to six o'clock this afternoon. Altar was decorated with Easter lilies, candles, and lights. Found it easy to pray, because I knew God had His eye on me. Prayed for Mom, Pop, the Beaver Chiefs, and myself. God must have been happy to see so many people in church today. At least, I did my part.

FRIDAY, April 7

Mom, Clara, and I went to church this afternoon. Saw some ladies crying while Father Foley was talking about the death of Jesus. Terry and Bo walked home with us. Am going to bed early.

SATURDAY, April 8

Had a busy day in the store. Eggs, eggs, eggs! Seemed as though everybody bought eggs. The old hens must be tired after laying all those eggs. Mrs. Clement told me that the rat poison killed four rats in her cellar. If you ask me, it's just as well that The Beaver Chief Rat Destroying Company, Incorporated, uncorporated. Mrs. Clement is like all women. She wanted results too quickly. Mr. Conlan gave me two dollars, because I worked extra hard. Mom pressed my suit and tie, and I shined my shoes. So, I'm all ready for tomorrow.

SUNDAY, April 9

Easter Sunday! Virginia Drake looked pretty nice in her new blue hat. Terry had a new suit, but mine looked just as good. Bet God was happy this morning when He saw so many people receiving Holy Communion. Mom, Pop, Clara, and I received Holy Communion at the nine o'clock Mass. Pop took the family uptown for breakfast. Went roller skating this afternoon with Terry and Virginia. Terry and I went to the movies tonight. Wonder what kind of a time Jean is having in New York! Bet she isn't even thinking about me.

MONDAY, April 10

Rented Clara's bicycle for a quarter. Froggie and I went riding in the country. Saw a man milking a cow and asked him if I could try it. I pulled the faucets, but no milk came out. Guess the cow knew that I was a stranger. Received a post card from Jean, a picture of Hotel Lexington. On the card were written these words:

X marks my room. Wish you were here.

JEAN WALLLACE

She must be having a pretty good time, when she couldn't find time to write more than that. Guess I'll read my mystery book called: "Ten Steps in the Dark."

TUESDAY, April 11
Father Foley phoned this morning and said that the second game for the championship will be played Friday night. The Beaver Chiefs tried to have a meeting in our garage, but Mom chased us. The Chiefs walked to Lake Shore Country Club, but we were too late to caddy. Took Virginia Drake to the movies tonight and, just as we turned into the "Lyric," we met Clint Tucker. Suppose Clint will tell Jean that I took Virginia to the movies. Well, Jean needn't think that I'm going to sit home, while she's having a good time in New York. That gives me an idea. Think I'll be nice to Virginia, and that will worry Jean.

WEDNESDAY, April 12
Went to the Lake Shore Country Club and had to wait for an hour before we had a chance to caddy. Terry, Froggie, Bo, and I caddied for four ladies. It

was awful — meaning the ladies. My lady couldn't hit the broad side of a cow. She took at least fifteen strokes on every hole. And such chatter! For four hours we had to hear about my maid, our bridge club, Mrs. Gilmore's new curtains, the stocking sale at Snyder's, how to make chiffon pie, the small sandwiches Mrs. Wright served at her tea, how hard it is to find a good maid, etc., etc., etc. No wonder women can't play golf. After playing nine holes, the ladies had lunch. We were hungry, too, but just had to suffer. For caddying eighteen holes and walking eighteen miles, my lady gave me seventy cents. Never, never, never again will I caddy for a woman! Women talk too much.

THURSDAY, April 13
Had another card from Jean saying:
Having the time of my life. Hope
you are having the same.

JEAN WALLACE

Jean will find out that I can have the time of my life without her. The team practiced this morning. Mrs. Drake hired me to clean her cellar this afternoon. She wanted to pay me, but I refused. Imagine me taking money from the mother of my best girl! Nothing doing! Some day I'll be cleaning Virginia's cellar, that is, after we are married. Mrs. Drake served a lunch and Virginia and I had a party. This was the best day of my vacation. Clint Tucker saw me leaving Virginia's house, but I don't care. Father Foley stopped at our house tonight. Mom asked him to come to supper next Wednesday night. He's coming.

FRIDAY, April 14

Poured rain. Had to stay in the house. Finished reading "Ten Steps in the Dark." Small crowd at the game tonight. The Beaver Chiefs beat the "Merry Madmen" by a score of 12 to 7, and now everybody is happy. Series stands one to one. Final game will be next Friday night. After the game Froggie was in an awful hurry: he said that he had to take care of something important. We found out that Sarah Connell was the "something important." We found Froggie and Sarah in Moulson's Drugstore drinking ice-cream sodas. Froggie must be in love, but why pick a girl in the seventh grade?

SATURDAY, April 15

Mom spent the whole day cleaning and getting ready for Father Foley. Why do people have to clean the whole house when they expect company? Father Foley will see only the dining room and parlor. Besides, Father Foley is coming to eat, not to look for dirt. After I came home from work, Mom made me clean the garage. Doesn't Mom know that Father Foley won't see the garage? Mom can certainly find excuses to keep me busy. Received a card from Jean saying:

Will arrive home Sunday at 5:10 p.m.

JEAN

Won't Jean be surprised when I don't meet her? Besides, I've a date with the best girl in the world, and her name is not Jean. It's Virginia.

SUNDAY, April 16

Aunt Sarah came for dinner and we had lamb, peas, white potatoes, and chocolate pie. Virginia and I went to see "The Clock Strikes." The other picture was "Between Two Loves," a story about a fellow with two girls. Kept thinking about myself all during the picture. After the show Virginia and I walked by the station. Mrs. Wallace, Jean, and Clint Tucker were just coming out of the station. Jean waved, but I pretended that I didn't see her. Am glad that Jean saw us. I'll bet Jean is worrying tonight.

MONDAY, April 17

Back to school. Jean Wallace tried to tell me about her trip to New York. Told her that I didn't care to hear anything about New York. When Jean saw that I was mad, she said: "Well, Pomp, I heard that you weren't very lonesome while I was away. Virginia Drake certainly took good care of you." I just laughed to myself. Guess Jean is worried all right.

TUESDAY, April 18

Class had election of officers today. Terry Mann was elected president. Mildred McCormick was elected vice-president. Margaret Hillard was elected secretary. Pompey Briggs was elected treasurer. Why, I don't know. Jean Wallace was made class prophet, because she writes good compositions. All officers had to make speeches. Father Foley gave us a class motto and it's a dandy — "Keep on keeping on!" Practiced for the final game on Friday night. Mom was as nervous as a bee tonight. She's worried about Father Foley coming tomorrow night. Mom's afraid that everything won't be right, and now she's sorry that she invited him. Had my usual talk on manners, which I always get just before company comes.

WEDNESDAY, April 19

Rained all day. Ate breakfast and lunch in the kitchen, because Mom had the dining-room table set for Father Foley. Had to take a bath after school, and it's only Wednesday. Father Foley brought Mom a picture of two farmers called "The Angelus." I spilled gravy on the tablecloth, but I don't think that Father Foley saw it. The Briggs family was certainly polite tonight. I never knew that we had so many manners. Guess it's just as well that Father Foley doesn't eat at our house every night. I could have eaten more, but had to be polite. Father Foley told Pop that he thought that I should go to college. Imagine a policeman going to college! Cider stole one of Father Foley's rubbers. Mom was mortified. We found the rubber under the kitchen table. Things always go wrong when we have company. That's why I don't like company. I like Father Foley though, except when he's company.

THURSDAY, April 20

Sister Agnes certainly wants the Beaver Chiefs to win the championship for Holy Cross. She said that she has been praying hard for us. That's what I call a friend. If I ever wanted anything, I want to win that game tomorrow night. Had a terrible fight with Clara. After supper I caught her in my room reading this diary. I wouldn't let anybody read this diary for a billion dollars, not even Virginia. Believe me, I pulled Clara's hair so hard that she'll never again read anybody's diary, especially, mine. Was sent to bed early.

FRIDAY, April 21

The Beaver Chiefs are the champions of the city. Score was 14 to 12. The "Merry Madmen" played a dirty game and had plenty of fouls called on them. Score was a tie with one minute to play. Terry threw the lucky basket. After the game everybody ran out on the floor to shake our hands. Virginia was so excited that she kissed me. Gosh, I felt ashamed. Imagine being kissed by a girl in front of all those people! I was so excited that, when Jean Wallace caught my hand, I forgot that I was mad at her. But now that the excitement is over, I'm going to start being mad again. Father Foley promised the Beaver Chiefs a party for next Wednesday night. Pomp Briggs feels mighty good tonight.

SATURDAY, April 22

Big piece in the paper about our winning the championship. It said some nice things about Holy Cross School and Father Foley. Cut the piece out of the paper and some day I'll show it to Pompey Junior. Mrs. Clement was in the store today and bought more rat poison. Mr. Nolan came in for his usual lunch. Yesterday a prisoner hit Mr. Nolan and he lost two teeth. Am beginning to think that being a policeman isn't so easy after all. Guess the water is hot, so I'll take my bath.

SUNDAY, April 23

Pop took the family for a ride. Stopped to visit Aunt Kate and Uncle Harry. Uncle Harry has a new calf, that is, Uncle Harry's cow has a new calf. This is the best time to live in the country. Trees are budding, birds are singing, and everything looks real countryish. Had two glasses of milk right from the cow. Supper at home. Bo came over after supper, and we took Virginia Drake and Mildred McCormick to the movies. While we were gone, Mrs. Wallace and Jean called on Mom. I'll bet Jean was mad, when Mom told her that I had taken Virginia to the show. Mrs. Wallace is going to run a card party for the church. She asked Mom to help her. Mom said that she would.

MONDAY, April 24

Now that the basketball season is over, the Beaver

Chiefs will have to have more meetings. Meeting called for tomorrow night.

TUESDAY, April 25

Burglars broke into Conlan's Grocery and stole one hundred and thirty-eight dollars. Poor Mr. Conlan! Stopped and told Mr. Conlan that I was sorry. The Beaver Chiefs held a short meeting tonight. Nobody paid dues, so I didn't pay mine. Everybody tried to talk at once, and that made things bad. Dick Burroughs took Clara to a dance tonight. Mom has sold fifteen tickets for the card party. Am still mad at Jean, and still like Virginia.

WEDNESDAY, April 26

Just came home from the Strand Hotel, where Father Foley had the party for the Beaver Chief Champions. All of our parents were there and we had a great time. Father Foley made a speech. He thanked the Beaver Chiefs for bringing the championship to Holy Cross and gave each one of us a belt and buckle. I'm going to wear mine with my Sunday pants. Mom and Pop were proud when Father Foley said those nice things about me. A man took a picture of the Beaver Chiefs. The picture will be in tomorrow's paper. Boy, won't Virginia be surprised to see my picture in the paper? And won't Jean be mad? Bet Jean will be sorry, because she's not my best girl.

THURSDAY, April 27

The picture of the Beaver Chief Champions appeared in tonight's *News*. There was a big piece about the banquet. Aunt Sarah phoned, and so did Virginia. Uncle Harry called from the country. Jean Wallace didn't call, and that makes me wonder.

FRIDAY, April 28

Clint Tucker's father has gone to work in Cleveland. The family will move there later. That means that Clint will not graduate with us. It means also that a certain Jean Wallace will be mighty lonesome. Now watch her shine up to Pompey Briggs. Mom has sold twenty-three tickets for the card party. I hope Mom sells a million tickets, because I like Father Foley. After supper Terry and I went for a walk. Saw a car with a Jersey license. Wonder if it was the car that took Mrs. Conway's rat for a ride!

SATURDAY, April 29

Business was poor today, but received my dollar and a quarter just the same. Mr. Nolan was in for lunch. Mrs. Clement bought some oranges but no rat poison. This is bath night, so Pomp's going to take his weekly swim.

SUNDAY, April 30

Mrs. Mann invited me for supper. Had hot dogs, potato salad, and chocolate cake. After supper Terry and

I went to see "The Road Turns," a good picture, but "The Glass Key" was better. Back to school tomorrow and that means more algebra. I'd like to meet the fellow who invented that stuff. He must have been dizzy, and we have to suffer.

MONDAY, May 1

Clint Tucker called me "Fats" today. On the way home from school I weighed myself. Gained seven pounds. Think I'll stop drinking milk, because nobody is going to call me "Fats." Besides, policemen don't have to be fat. They never put fat policemen on Main Street and that's where I want to be — near the picture shows. Mom and Clara are at the hall getting ready for the card party. Mom wants me to help with the checking. Hope they don't forget me when they serve the ice cream and cake.

TUESDAY, May 2

Card party was a big success. Had plenty of fun checking, and made only a few mistakes. Mrs. Wallace and Mom cleared one hundred and twenty-one dollars on the party. Boy, I was glad to see Father Foley so happy. Every time Jean Wallace came near the checking booth, I pretended that I was busy. Girls never know their place.

WEDNESDAY, May 3

I've just been wondering. Tomorrow will be my birthday. When I mentioned it at supper, no one said anything. Mom hasn't been uptown lately, and it looks as though Pomp is going to be out of luck. Birthdays were made for presents and they should know that around this house.

THURSDAY, May 4

Fourteen years old today! Nobody mentioned my birthday and I was mad all day. About five o'clock Mom sent me on an errand to Aunt Sarah's. Found the eighth grade waiting there with a surprise party. Mom, Pop, and Clara came later, and we had a great time. Mom made Jean Wallace sit next to me at the table. Something tells me that Jean is nicer than I thought. Aunt Sarah had plenty of ice cream and a cake with fourteen candles. Terry made a speech and the class gave me three cheers. Yes, it was a swell birthday except that it didn't last long enough.

FRIDAY, May 5

Deemer Weston has a new suit. It's about time that he shed the short pants. Pop bought four tickets for the American Legion Minstrel Show, which will be held at the Palace Theater next Thursday night. Jean phoned to tell me that she had a good time at my party. Guess Jean is pretty good after all. What's the use of being mad at someone? Most of the time the other person doesn't know how mad you are.

SATURDAY, May 6

The Beaver Chiefs went on a May walk, but the President had to work. Business was very poor today. When Mr. Conlan paid me, he told me that I would not have to work during the summer months, so, today was my last day in the store until next September. It would happen just when I need money to buy clothes for graduation. That's always the way with things in this world. Seems as though you can't plan on anything except Saturday night baths, one of which I'm going to take right now.

SUNDAY, May 7

Clara let me take her bike, and Froggie and I went for a ride in East Park. Stopped at the pavilion and had coffee and doughnuts. Froggie tore his pants in the sprocket of his wheel. I went into the house with him, because we figured that his mother wouldn't say much in front of me. We were wrong. Froggie's mother scolded and said plenty. Aunt Sarah came for supper. After supper the Briggs family played "rummy" for matches.

MONDAY, May 8

Clara had a "shower" tonight for Sylvia Dalton who will be married soon. All the girls brought presents for Sylvia. Clara wouldn't let me see the presents, because they were "personal things" — whatever that means. Wonder if they have "showers" for men who are going to be policemen! There's an idea. The girls are singing "Sweet Adeline," so I'm going to bed.

TUESDAY, May 9

Mrs. Wallace is sick. Stopped after school and Jean gave me a piece of apple pie which she made this afternoon. If anybody ever asks you who makes the best apple pie in the world, just say that my girl is the champion. Some day Jean will be making pies for me. Just happened to think. . . . Suppose somebody should find this diary and read it! Well, I'm going to hide it, where no one will find it. This diary is like Sylvia Dalton's presents — it's personal.

WEDNESDAY, May 10

Mrs. Wallace is still sick. Weather warm. Nothing happened.

THURSDAY, May 11

Just came home from the American Legion Minstrel Show. Laughed so much I split my heels. Mom liked the singing, Pop liked the jokes, and Clara was too nice to like anything. There were three acrobats, a couple of tap dancers, a banjoist, and a magician. The magician put a watch in a handkerchief, threw the handkerchief into the air, and out came a dove. Then he put a woman into a wooden box and sawed the box in half. It looked as though the magician had sawed the woman in half. When the box was put together again, out walked the woman. Boy, that was a great trick. When the magician called for volunteers, Mart Hanna and I went on the stage. The magician showed the audience that there was nothing in my pockets. After shooting a gun into the air, the magician put his hands into my pockets and took out a pigeon, playing cards, handkerchiefs, underwear, a hammer, and a gold watch. Gosh, I was scared! I can't figure out how he did that trick. Then the magician put a girl to sleep, raised her body off the ground, and the girl slept in the air. He was the best magician I ever saw. I bought one of his books for a quarter. It's called: "How to Be a Magician in Twenty Easy Lessons." *I'm going to be a magician.*

FRIDAY, May 12
Mrs. Wallace was better today. The Beaver Chiefs held a special meeting to initiate Bert Chamberlain. Bert knows tonight that he's an honest-to-goodness Beaver Chief. Boy, how he yelled when we paddled him! Bought Mom some candy for Mother's Day. Can't write much tonight, because I want to read "How to Be a Magician in Twenty Easy Lessons."

SATURDAY, May 13
Slept until ten-thirty. Rented Clara's bike and Froggie and I went for a ride. I can't figure Froggie lately. Think he's turning sissy. Froggie made me help him pick some flowers. He said he wanted them for his mother. Just before supper Clara saw him going into Sarah Connell's house with flowers. I'll bet they were the ones we picked! Imagine Froggie taking flowers to that seventh-grade baby! If people fall in love in the spring, then Froggie's in love. Guess I'll take my bath.

SUNDAY, May 14

Mother's Day! Couldn't go to church. Woke up with swollen face, hands, and legs. Mom said that it was "poison ivy." That came from picking flowers for Froggie's best girl. Boy, but I look messy tonight, just like the fat man in the circus. I've itched so much that it's a wonder my bones haven't jumped out of my skin. Pop rubbed me with alcohol and now I have to take a bath in Epsom salts. Looks as though last night's bath was wasted. Mom liked the candy. Couldn't have any myself, because candy is bad for a person with poison ivy.

MONDAY, May 15

No school for me today. Still bloated, and still messy.

TUESDAY, May 16

Felt better today, but had plenty of itches. Froggie called after school. He wasn't poisoned at all. When I asked Froggie how Sarah Connell liked his flowers, his face became as red as a beet. Mrs. Drake sent me a cake. Have to take another bath tonight in Epsom salts. Gosh, when I return to school, the Beaver Chiefs won't know their president.

WEDNESDAY, May 17

Poison ivy has gone. Felt pretty good today. Mom wouldn't let me go to school, so I studied "How to Be a Magician in Twenty Easy Lessons." Practiced some of the tricks, but they didn't work. Terry and Bo called after school. Mrs. Tucker and Clint are going to move to Cleveland next week. I want to thank Mr. Tucker for being so good to me. Now somebody worth while can be nice to Jean Wallace without interference. Tomorrow will be Ascension Thursday. No school. Class is going on a May walk. Mom said that I could go, if I'll keep away from the poison ivy. I will.

THURSDAY, May 18

Class had May walk. Walked to Brewer's Grove. Just as we started to eat our lunch, Mr. Brewer chased us. We didn't know that we were supposed to pay to use his Grove! Anyway, it wasn't so good in the Grove — too many flies. Finally went to East Park where we ate in the pavilion. Clint Tucker was overnice to Jean Wallace. It made me mad, but I can stand it for a few more days. Anyway, I had lunch with Virginia Drake. Froggie wants to have another May walk and invite the seventh grade. I think I know the reason. The reason is Sarah Connell.

FRIDAY, May 19

On the way home from school I found Froggie's algebra book in front of Mrs. Decker's house. Inside the book I found a note. I know that it's wrong to read another's note, but no one will read this diary, so I copied the note for myself. Here's what it said:

My Dearest Froggie:

While you were on the May walk yesterday, I was very lonesome. I tried to read a book, but kept thinking about you. If you didn't have a good time, then I'll know that you are my best fellow. Why don't you stop at our house about five o'clock on Sunday afternoon? Perhaps, my mother will invite you for supper.

Your best girl,

SARAH CONNELL

SATURDAY, May 20

Gave Froggie his algebra book, but didn't say anything about Sarah's note. Rained most of the afternoon. Dick Burroughs took Clara to the movies tonight. Guess I'll go to bed early, because I'm going to have a big day tomorrow.

SUNDAY, May 21

Walked to church with Mrs. Drake and Virginia. After supper Terry, Bo, Ted Conway, and I went over to Sarah Connell's house and peeked through the window. At the dining-room table sat Froggie with the Connell family. We gave a boy a nickel to ring Connell's doorbell. When Mrs. Connell came to the door, the boy gave her an envelope which we had written to Froggie. Inside the envelope was this letter:

SPECIAL NOTE TO FROGGIE

If you don't stop hanging around the cradle of that

seventh-grade girl, you will be expelled from the Society of the Beaver Chiefs.

THE MEMBERS OF THE BEAVER CHIEFS

We hid in the bushes and watched Froggie as he read our note. After he read it, Froggie took his hat and left for home. Oh boy, I'll bet he was mad.

MONDAY, May 22
The Chiefs wanted to have a special meeting to expel Froggie, but I wouldn't stand for it. Froggie is too good a fellow. Froggie told me about the note this afternoon and made me promise that I wouldn't tell anybody. Froggie thinks that Clint Tucker wrote the note. Of course, if Froggie wants to think that way, far be it from me to change his thinking. If he wants to fall in love with a seventh-grade girl, why, he can't help what his heart does to him. Some day when I grow up, I'll tell him who wrote that note.

TUESDAY, May 23
Froggie, Terry, and I skipped school and went to the opening ball game. Met everybody whom we didn't want to meet, even Father Foley. Boy, we'll catch it tomorrow. Now, if I were a first-class magician, I could have been in school and at the ball game at the same time. Mom bought Cider a new collar. I'd better get lots of sleep tonight. I'll need it when things start to pop tomorrow.

WEDNESDAY, May 24

Froggie, Terry, and I were sent to the Principal for skipping school. The Principal sent us to Father Foley. Father Foley said that we had given bad example and had no honor. He was mad at first, but it isn't Father Foley to be mad. We said that we were sorry, and Father Foley talked about the ball game and treated us to chocolate candy. We promised not to skip school again for an opening ball game. That promise will be easy to keep, because there'll be no more opening ball games this year.

THURSDAY, May 25

Mom went to the cooking school at the Palace Theater this afternoon. Mom had a lucky number and won a tin of biscuits. The biscuits were good, but not as good as Mom's. That's one thing that my wife will have to do well — make good biscuits. After supper Bo and I went to the "Lyric" to see "Thrice Foiled" and "The Road to Yesterday." Just two mushy pictures with a lot of kissing. No Mickey Mouse!

FRIDAY, May 26

Clint Tucker's last day at Holy Cross! Even though Clint did get into my ankles, still I hated to see him leave us. Forgave him for the many times he stole Jean Wallace from me. Jean cried in front of the whole class. Guess she liked Clint all right. Mrs. Tucker and Clint left for Cleveland tonight on the seven o'clock train. Jean and I went to the station. Just before he left, Clint kissed Jean. Felt like clipping him, but held on, because I'll never see him again. Jean cried on the way home and didn't have much to say. I treated her to some ice cream, and then she began to feel better. Things look better for me with Clint Tucker out of the way.

SATURDAY, May 27

Helped Mom clean the cellar. Listened to the radio and studied "How to Be a Magician in Twenty Easy Lessons." Learned a card trick which I'll show to the Beaver Chiefs next week.

SUNDAY, May 28

Father Foley gave a great talk today. He told us how Christ gave His Mother to us. In other words, we have two mothers. Even though we can't see the Blessed Virgin Mary, she is right by our sides, helping us to do things and keeping us from sin. That's something that I'm going to remember. Father Foley said that Mary always gets her friends into heaven. If that's so, then I'm going to be one of Mary's best friends. I'm going to tie on to Mary's apron string, because I want to get to heaven. Mrs. Wallace and Jean called tonight. Caught Jean looking at me several times. If looks mean anything, Jean Wallace likes me.

MONDAY, May 29

Virginia Drake has a new dress. Gosh, the more I

looked at her today, the more I thought that she should be my best girl. Wonder if Pop ever had two girls at the same time! Wouldn't I have liked to have seen Pop and Mom walking home from school! All fellows do those things, and Pop must have been just like the rest of the fellows. Some day I'm going to ask Aunt Sarah about Pop.

TUESDAY, May 30

Decoration Day! No school. This morning the Beaver Chiefs watched the parade. Pop marched and the Beaver Chiefs gave him a big hand. We clapped hard for the Civil War veterans. Wouldn't it be great to have one of those veterans sitting next to you during history exam? The family went to Aunt Sarah's for dinner. After dinner Pop took us for a ride to Litchfield Falls. Too many people there, so we didn't stay long. Sat on the porch for the first time this summer. The family went to East Park tonight to watch the fireworks. The "Niagara Falls" piece was the best on the program. Came home about eleven o'clock. Pomp's going to bed.

WEDNESDAY, May 31

Sister Agnes wants our graduation to be tops. Well, if Sister Agnes will pass us in the exams, we'll do our part. Began to practice for the graduation entertainment today. The eighth-grade boys will have a dumbbell drill. Inside of the dumbbells will be electric lights, and we will do our drill in the dark. The audience will not see us, only our clubs swinging in the air. Sounds pretty good to me. The girls will put on a play called: "At the End of the Rainbow." Virginia Drake will play the leading part. Jean Wallace will take the part of a society girl, and I'll bet that she'll do a good job. After school the Beaver Chiefs watched the men putting up signs for the circus. This year's circus will be bigger than ever. I want to see the fellow who swallows the swords. Wonder how he does it! Maybe, he's a magician. Some day Pompey Briggs will have his picture on billboards. People will pay money to see Pompey Briggs — the greatest magician of all times. Won't that be something?

THURSDAY, June 1

Jean Wallace received a letter from Clint Tucker. Jean let me read the letter. Clint said that he is very lonesome and that there is a big hole in his heart. Such mush! The Principal in the Cleveland school said that Clint will not be able to graduate until next January. It takes smart fellows like us to graduate in June. Clint ended his letter with a lot of X's and that pleased Jean. Boy, if Clint Tucker ever knew that I read his letter, he'd tear me to pieces. Clint will find out that, after Jean becomes Mrs. Pompey Briggs, I won't allow him to write letters to my wife. Class had a meeting and decided to have Class Day Exercises two weeks from today. Jean has begun work on the class prophecy. Sylvia Dalton will be married Saturday. The whole family will be going to the wedding.

FRIDAY, June 2

Things have been very quiet around here until this morning. Last night Pop left his bridgework on the kitchen table, and this morning the teeth were gone. We looked high and low, but couldn't find them. Pop stormed and raved, and had to go to work without his teeth and without his usual breakfast. Mom found the teeth under the icebox. Pop wanted to whip Cider tonight, but Mom wouldn't let him. Suppose Cider thought that the teeth were a new kind of bone. Bet Pop'll take his teeth to bed with him in the future. That's what he should do. That's what I do.

SATURDAY, June 3

Wore my best clothes to Sylvia Dalton's wedding. It certainly took Sylvia a long time to get married. I thought that we'd never get out of the church. Mom gave me a bag of rice to throw on the bride for good luck. Everybody was throwing rice and having a grand time. When nobody was looking, I threw my bag of rice, hit Mr. Beemer's stovepipe hat, and made a hole in it. Mr. Beemer was as mad as a wet hen. I heard him tell Mrs. Crane that, if he knew who ruined his new hat, he would hang the culprit by the heels. I just looked kind of pious and Mr. Beemer never suspected me. Sylvia Dalton had enough rice without mine. The Briggs family went to the reception tonight. Had four pieces of cake and three dishes of ice cream. Pop drank four glasses of wine, and he giggled and laughed all the way home. Mom kept saying: "Chester Briggs, I'm mortified. Chester Briggs, I'm mortified." Then Pop would laugh and giggle some more. Pop told me that he thought that it was a great wedding. I agree with him.

SUNDAY, June 4

It beats all how fast these Sundays come around. It always takes a long time for Saturday to come, and when it does come, it never lasts very long. Can't have much fun on Sunday. Rained this afternoon. Pop wasn't feeling very well. He said that he had too much wedding. I couldn't figure what he meant, because Pop didn't get married. After supper Terry and I went for a walk. Terry said that, when he grows up, he's going to be a trumpet player in a band. I'm going to be a magician, the world's greatest magician. When I'm a magician, perhaps, I'll be able to do something about these Sundays coming so often. Maybe, I'll change the Sundays into Saturdays.

MONDAY, June 5

A month from today I won't have to study algebra. That will be something. Father Foley is going to take the Beaver Chiefs to the circus on Thursday. I always knew that Father Foley was tops, but just at present he is the best of the best. That means no school for the Beaver Chiefs on Thursday afternoon. Sister Agnes said that the rest of the class could have a party. Hope Jean writes and tells Clint Tucker that the

Beaver Chiefs are going to the circus. Steak and onions for supper, and chocolate cake!

TUESDAY, June 6

After supper I found a letter in the hall. Of course, I had to look at it, even though it is wrong to read another's letter. It was a note from Dick Burroughs to Clara. The note read:

DEAREST APPLE PIE:

I had to write to you tonight, because I am so lonesome. I wish you could see me more often. Each minute away from you is an eternity. Don't forget our date for Friday night! I'll be waiting at the same place at the usual time. Do take care of yourself, because you are so precious.

With lots of love,

DICK

Gave the letter to Clara and said nothing. I'll bet she thinks that I read her letter.

WEDNESDAY, June 7

Walked home from school with Jean Wallace. We met Froggie and his Sarah near the Carter Street playground. This love bug is certainly biting the Beaver Chiefs. Mom pressed my good suit, so that I can wear it to the circus tomorrow. Clara is mad at me, because she thinks that I read her letter. I suppose I'd be mad too, if anybody ever read this diary. But nobody will ever see this diary. I'll guard it with my life. Mom often asks me, what I'm doing upstairs every night. I tell her that I'm improving myself. Mom thinks that I'm studying, and far be it from me to change her thinking.

THURSDAY, June 8

Rained all morning and it looked bad for the circus. Father Foley said that it always rains on circus day. Had seats right in the middle of the tent. Saw two men shot from a cannon. Didn't like the fellow who swallowed the swords — he made me sick. Some elephants danced, and some bears roller-skated. The clowns were great. Laughed so much that the tears rolled down my cheeks. Father Foley liked the acrobats, and I did too, especially, when the fellow missed the swing and fell into the net. Think it would have been better, if they hadn't used a net. Father Foley treated us to hot dogs and lemonade. Tomorrow will be the fifteenth anniversary of Father Foley's ordination. The Beaver Chiefs are going to buy cigars for him. Now, if I were a magician, I could buy a barrel of cigars for Father Foley. He deserves them. Yes, it was a swell circus.

FRIDAY, June 9

The Beaver Chiefs gave the cigars to Father Foley. He thanked us and said that we should not have bought them, but we know better. That's what I like — surprising people when they don't expect it. Had a long practice for the entertainment this afternoon, and our drill is coming along fine. We watched the girls practice too. Virginia Drake was fine, and so was Jean Wallace. Practiced some of my card tricks tonight, because I want to be a good magician, the World's Best Magician.

SATURDAY, June 10

Had to cut the grass this morning and clean the windows. Mom gave me half a dollar. This afternoon Terry and I saw Froggie carrying a basket of groceries for Sarah Connell. Froggie pretended that he didn't see us, but we'll tell him about it tomorrow. Clara is still mad. When Dick Burroughs called this evening, he didn't look any too friendly, especially, when I called Clara "Apple Pie." Why is it that when people fall in love, it always goes to their heads? Oh well, I'll take a bath and call it a day.

SUNDAY, June 11

The Beaver Chiefs received Holy Communion in a body. We offered our Communions for Father Foley's intention. That made something extra for his fifteenth anniversary. When we told Father Foley, he was very happy. Terry and I walked home from church with Jean and Virginia. Jean has written the class prophecy, but wouldn't tell what she has written about us. Had a special rehearsal this afternoon, and our drill was perfect. Terry came over after supper and we went to the movies. Nothing else happened.

MONDAY, June 12

Sister Agnes gave us a fine talk this morning. Told us to be always loyal to God and Holy Cross Church. Asked the class to pray for her often and we all promised. That will be easy, because Sister Agnes has been pretty good to the Beaver Chiefs. Father Foley gave us plans for graduation. Jean Wallace will be the valedictorian. I'll have to give a speech of welcome. Cider followed me to school this afternoon and Sister made me take him home. Mom bought me a new suit of clothes, a white shirt, a tie, and a pair of sport shoes. Looks as though graduation will be something extra special in the life of Pompey Briggs.

TUESDAY, June 13

Reviewed for the exams. What a headache! Father Foley gave me my speech, and it is a honey — not too many big words, and not too long. I'm going to make the Beaver Chiefs proud of their president on graduation night. Brought my seventy-five cents for the Class Day banquet. Father Foley has chartered a bus and we are going to Glen Carron for the day. Will have dinner at the hotel. Can't write much tonight, because I have to learn my speech.

WEDNESDAY, June 14

Algebra drill all morning. Spent most of the afternoon practicing for the entertainment. Our drill was perfect. "At the End of the Rainbow" was fine, especially, when Jean and Virginia were on the stage. Father Foley heard my speech and spent an hour helping me to improve. Pop went to the American Legion banquet tonight, and had to wear a stiff shirt with one of those funny collars. Boy, how he carried on trying to get his tie in shape. Gee, if I were a magician, I could have fixed the tie by just snapping my fingers. There's a good business for somebody — tying people's ties when they go to banquets — a professional tie tier.

THURSDAY, June 15

Class Day was good and bad. Bus left school for Glen Carron at nine o'clock. Had plenty of fun in the bus. The Beaver Chiefs beat a scrub team in baseball. Swell dinner at the hotel. Father Foley made a speech and told us to "keep on keeping on." Jean's class prophecy was great. Jean said that Froggie would be a doctor, Bo an aviator, Terry a professor, and Virginia a nurse. I liked what Jean said about me, but I wish that she hadn't said it before the class. Jean said that some day I would be married to Miss Jean Wallace, and that made the class roar. Poor Virginia blushed. After dinner we had games and races. In the three-legged race, Virginia was running with Katie Barron. Both of them fell, and Virginia broke her arm. That put a damper on Class Day, and Father Foley made us start for home. Father Foley took Virginia and her mother to the hospital. Virginia's arm will have to be in a cast for six weeks. That means that she will not play the lead in the play, "At the End of the Rainbow." It's too bad the accident happened just before graduation. I'll say a prayer for Virginia tonight.

FRIDAY, June 16

Sister Agnes cried when Virginia walked into the classroom this morning. Virginia proved to be a pretty good soldier. She didn't cry, not even when Sister Agnes announced that Helen Brady would play Virginia's part in the play, "At the End of the Rainbow." Father Foley said plenty of nice things about Virginia and we all clapped. If I had had the chance, I could have said more nice things about Virginia. I know Virginia better than Father Foley does, and, besides, Virginia is my second best girl. Jean Wallace was swell to Virginia and offered to help her in every way. Gee, now I don't know which girl I like. I liked Jean a lot today, and I seemed to like Virginia more than ever. Having two girls makes my heart jump flips.

SATURDAY, June 17

Had to cut the grass this morning and help Pop clean the garage. Jean Wallace and Terry Mann came over this afternoon. They had a basket of sweets that they were taking to Virginia. Mom added a jar of black currant jam and an apple pie. Jean, Terry, and I then went to Virginia's house. Virginia was certainly happy, and tears trickled down her cheeks. Stayed there most of the afternoon and Virginia's mother gave us a lunch. I went to Terry's house for supper and had baked beans, brown bread, and apple kuchen. Could have eaten another piece of kuchen, but was ashamed after eating three pieces. Aunt Sarah came over tonight and I tried on my graduation suit. Aunt Sarah said that I'll be the best looking boy on the stage. We'll see.

SUNDAY, June 18

Practiced for the entertainment this afternoon. Caught Virginia Drake crying while the girls were practicing "At the End of the Rainbow." Felt so bad that I could have cried too. Helen Brady was fair in Virginia's part, but she'll never come up to Virginia. After rehearsal Froggie and I walked home with Jean and Virginia. We stopped at Moulson's Drugstore for a soda. Who should come in but Sarah Connell! Froggie blushed from head to toes. Froggie asked Sarah to have a soda, but Sarah refused. Gosh, how I laughed to myself. I'll bet Froggie was worried. Well, Sarah Connell needn't think that Froggie will steal Jean or Virginia, because I have my eye on both of them. Tomorrow we start the big week. I have been waiting nine months for graduation week, and now I'm sorry that it's here.

MONDAY, June 19

Had exam in silent reading this morning, and it was hard. Had history exam this afternoon, and it was easy. Received our tickets for graduation. Have seven reserved seats for Mom, Pop, Clara, Dick Burroughs, Aunt Sarah, Aunt Kate, and Uncle Harry. Sister Agnes placed us on the stage and I had to give my speech before the class. The Beaver Chiefs said that my speech was pretty good. I hope that they were telling the truth. Jean Wallace was perfect in her valedictory. Clara was very friendly tonight. Suppose she wants to be proud of me on Friday. Well, I'm going to make the whole family proud that they know Pompey Briggs. I'll hypnotize them, even though I'm not a first-class magician.

TUESDAY, June 20

After all my worry about x, y, z, the algebra exam was a song. Had our test in commercial arithmetic this afternoon, and the exams are finished. Sister Agnes said that she'll tell us tomorrow, whether or not we'll graduate. Well, Pompey Briggs had better graduate, because I have all my clothes. Mom bought a new dress this afternoon, and Clara bought a new hat. Looks as though the Briggs family will take no back seats. Terry, Bo, Froggie, and I celebrated tonight by going to the movies. Gosh, it doesn't seem as though graduation is so near. Kind of wish that it wasn't coming. However, the Beaver Chiefs can't stay in school all their lives. We have to "keep on keeping on." Besides, I have to be a magician.

WEDNESDAY, June 21

The whole class passed. We almost tore down the school when Sister Agnes told us the news. Spent most of the day practicing and had plenty of fun, because everybody was happy. When I told the good news to Mom, she kissed me — something that Mom hasn't done in a long, long time. Pop made a speech. "Pomp," said Pop, "we're proud of you. You've traveled over a hard road and the end has brought you victory. When they place the laurel wreath on your head at graduation, hold your head high, because that wreath means victory." A laurel wreath! Who wants a laurel wreath? What I want is a diploma. Mrs. Wallace and Jean came over after supper, and all night long we talked graduation, graduation, graduation. Mom made sandwiches and coffee, and brought out some of her extra special chocolate cake. It was a nice little party, but would have been better if Virginia had been there. Think I'll go to bed and practice my speech to myself, because I don't want to forget it.

THURSDAY, June 22

Had my hair cut this morning. After supper we had our final practice for graduation. After the rehearsal Terry, Bo, Froggie, Ted Conway, Jean, Virginia, and I talked for an hour on the corner of Payne Street. Talked about the good times we have had at Holy Cross School. Guess they all feel just as I do tonight — sorry that the end is here. Tomorrow will be the end of eight long years, eight years spent with the best friends in the world. We've had our fights and quarrels, but none of them was serious. Gee, wouldn't it be great if we could "keep on keeping on," if we could keep right on just as we have for the past eight years! Boy, I'm glad that I kept this diary. After our wedding I'll show this diary to Jean. Then, we can live again our happy days at Holy Cross.

FRIDAY, June 23

Graduation Day — the happiest day of my life! Felt mighty swell with all my new clothes. Before the entertainment the class gave Sister Agnes a black bag. She tried to thank us, but was so happy that she cried. We clapped and cheered, and Sister shook our hands. Hall was crowded. Guess everybody in Blackford came to see us graduate. My speech opened the program. Was nervous at first, but made no mistakes. Mom and Pop said that I surprised them. The audience liked our drill so well that we had to give it twice: the people clapped, and clapped, and clapped. Jean Wallace was great in the play "At the End of the Rainbow," and her valedictory was a masterpiece. Graduation followed the entertainment. Boy, how the people clapped when Father Foley read our names for diplomas. There were no laurel wreaths and I was mighty glad. When Virginia Drake's name was called, the audience almost tore the roof off the hall. Virginia looked lovely, even though her arm was in a cast. The whole class rose as a tribute to Virginia, and she deserved it. Father Foley said that we were the best class that had ever graduated from Holy Cross School, and I agree with him. Father Foley told us to keep close to God and to "keep on keeping on." Jean Wallace won the scholarship medal and Helen Rogers won the attendance medal. The singing of the "Alma Mater" closed the program. Guess everybody in Blackford shook hands with me. Mom invited Mrs. Wallace, Mrs. Drake, Jean, and Virginia to the house for a party. Had a grand time until twelve-thirty. Mom and Pop gave me five dollars and Aunt Sarah gave me a dollar. Clara and Dick Burroughs gave me a billfold. Aunt Kate and Uncle Harry gave me a fountain pen. Virginia gave me a rose, and Jean gave me a carnation. Put the rose, the carnation, and our graduation program in the fly leaf of my dictionary. Boy, oh boy, it was a great night, and I'm happy. Pop seemed proud tonight. Mom was all smiles, but there was a tear in her eye. I wonder why!

*　*　*

TWO LETTERS

726 WESTMORELAND DRIVE
CLEVELAND, OHIO
APRIL 8, 1963

Mr. Pompey Briggs
c/o The Pastor of Holy Cross Church
Holy Cross Rectory
Blackford, N. Y.

DEAR POMPEY:

This morning's mail brought me a pleasant surprise — an invitation to attend the Golden Jubilee celebration of Holy Cross Church in Blackford. That invitation has stirred up pleasant memories of my boyhood — Holy Cross, Father Foley, Sister Agnes, and all the rest. I have been wondering how my friends have fared during the past twenty-three years. My wondering has urged me to write this letter.

You will be pleased to learn that I have been married to a Cleveland girl, Elizabeth Hogan, and God has blessed us with two fine sons and a daughter. I am in the insurance business and have been very successful.

Are you planning to attend the Golden Jubilee celebration? If so, let me know, and I will certainly be on hand.

I am sending this letter to the Pastor of Holy Cross and am asking him to forward the letter to you. With every good wish, I am

Your old friend,
CLINTON TUCKER

Mr. Clinton Tucker
736 Westmoreland Drive
Cleveland, Ohio

DEAR CLINT:

Your letter arrived this morning and I assure you that it has given me a great deal of pleasure.

Yes, I am planning to attend the Golden Jubilee celebration of Holy Cross. I have tickets for the banquet and shall expect you to be my guest. Plan to spend a few days with me at Dunlap. It will be good for both of us.

You will be surprised to learn that Father Foley is still Pastor of Holy Cross. That means that we must attend the celebration. Won't Father Foley be surprised to see us?

Of course, we will visit the school where our old friend, Sister Agnes, is still teaching carpeting, papering, and algebra. I wonder if her smile is as broad as ever!

No doubt, you will welcome news regarding some of your former friends. Bo Parker, now known as Dr. George Parker, is a prominent physician in New York City. His monthly lectures at Doctors' Hospital are well attended.

If you are a movie fan, then you have seen Terry Mann on the screen. Yes, Don Mann is our old Beaver

Chief friend, Terry. His next picture will be titled: "Good Morning, Mr. Midnight!"

Our friend, Froggie Allen, married Sarah Connell. They have three girls and one boy. By the way, their son is named Pompey Allen. How do you like that?

Spring Brings Romance, the latest best seller, has been authored by Ted Conway. You will enjoy reading it, especially, after knowing the author.

Fourteen years ago I lost my father, and five years ago I lost my mother. Both rest side by side in Holy Cross Cemetery. May God be good to their souls!

My sister, Clara, married Dick Burroughs. They live in St. Louis, where Dick runs a gas station. Clara is busy mothering two fine children.

About ten years ago, Clint, I ran across an article in the *New York Herald Tribune* which stated that Virginia Drake had been voted the most popular stewardess of the American Airways. The article contained a picture of Virginia and said that her charming personality had won for her the coveted title of "The Most Popular Bluebird of the Air."

I suppose you are wondering about Jean Wallace. Well, Jean married a lawyer, Harold Flynn, about eight years ago. They are living in Cincinnati and have four children. We always exchange cards at Christmas time.

As for myself, Clint, I am still single, but very happy. President, banker, policeman, magician — these were my ambitions in youth, the dreams that have never been realized. As I think of them now, they cause me to smile.

The years have been kind to me, Clint, and God has been very good. God has been close to me. God has been my friend. What more could I ask?

You know, Clint, very often people walk into our lives to influence us when we least suspect it. Well, that happened to me. In my early days at Holy Cross, Father Foley walked into my life and became my idol and hero. Down through the years Father Foley has remained my idol and my hero.

When we meet at the Golden Jubilee celebration in Blackford, you will call me "Pomp." That title, however, I have discarded for a more worthy one. May I always be worthy of my new title — Reverend Pompey Briggs!

Sincerely in Christ,

POMPEY BRIGGS